The Hotel Lincoln

Also by Zephyros Major:

The Shovel Revival: A Motorcycle Manifesto

The Hotel Lincoln

A Novel

Zephyros Major

iUniverse, Inc.
New York Bloomington Shanghai

The Hotel Lincoln

Copyright © 2008 by Zephyros Major

All rights reserved. No part of this book may be used or reproduced by any means, graphic, electronic, or mechanical, including photocopying, recording, taping or by any information storage retrieval system without the written permission of the publisher except in the case of brief quotations embodied in critical articles and reviews.

iUniverse books may be ordered through booksellers or by contacting:

iUniverse
1663 Liberty Drive
Bloomington, IN 47403
www.iuniverse.com
1-800-Authors (1-800-288-4677)

Because of the dynamic nature of the Internet, any Web addresses or links contained in this book may have changed since publication and may no longer be valid.

This is a work of fiction. All of the characters, names, incidents, organizations, and dialogue in this novel are either the products of the author's imagination or are used fictitiously.

ISBN: 978-0-595-48618-2 (pbk)
ISBN: 978-0-595-71998-3 (cloth)
ISBN: 978-0-595-60712-9 (ebk)

Printed in the United States of America

Cultivo una rosa blanca
En julio como en enero
Para el amigo sincero
Que me da su mano franca
—*Jose Marti*

Habanamera, guajira Habanamera....

Day 1

Gabrel Sourdough stepped out of the bright, air-conditioned airport terminal into the sweltering, black night with two things on his mind: a flat bed and a strong drink. He had spent most of the last twenty-four hours in transit, contorting his frame to fit the seats in the waiting areas and on the planes along the way, with little success catching up on sleep. Now miraculously, painlessly through customs, there seemed little reason to remain so highly on guard and nervous. He took a deep breath, and prepared for the onslaught of drivers.

They swarmed around him like bees starved for pollen, around the only flower left untapped, shouting and elbowing and pointing to their cars and trying to wrestle the ensemble—a large black pack with a smaller, more mobile, detachable version latched to it—from his back all at once. The behavior was the same, as if scripted, outside every airport Sourdough had passed through in all of Latin America; you see white skin, you charge toward it. The drivers did not seem to realize how their disorganization cancelled each other out, how their yelling turned him off, how their attempts at French, Italian, German and English—trying to guess the turista's origins—only worked against their interests.

It was more of a choreographed dance than a business negotiation. There was no denying that they were twenty to thirty kilometers outside of town. Gabrel would need a ride. He would need to choose one of them. They knew it true as well as he did. Yet his proven technique of avoiding eye contact, looking beyond them, over their heads, or knowingly off into the distance as though familiar with the surroundings did the job of thinning the throng. He ignored them, walking away, taking a cigarette out of a pack purchased for just such an occasion, determining not to say a word, not to acknowledge a soul until he'd puffed it down to the filter and smothered it under his sandal. The scene was worth reflecting on, anyhow. He was standing on Cuban ground.

Equipped with local coin, a phone card, and a Bible-sized guidebook complete with addresses to casa particulars, Sourdough finally picked a man with heavy wrinkles framing a considerably dishonest face. He chose this man because he knew he could never grow too relaxed, or become too trusting, of such a devilish demeanor. And he wagered the driver was aware of his revealing characteristics, which is why both parties participated in the ride's conversation with cautious, respect-filled honesty.

"Necessito un casa particular, por favor."

"Donde?"

Sourdough consulted the city map in the guidebook. "La Capitolo. Habana Centro, por favor."

"Si, si. Tengo."

"Tienne? Cuantos? Donde?"

"Tengo, tengo."

It was two-thirty in the morning. The driver made a cell phone call as they zoomed into Habana, swerving by a curb to pick up another man just as the grandly-lit Capitolo came into view. The new figure sat in the front, clearly the voice on the other end of the phone call, turned with a nod, a sheepish "Hel-lo", and they were off again, streaking past the old parliament, down a lightless alley, halting in front of a door like any other, but with a sticker displaying the logo of a stick-drawn house slapped in the window, much to Gabrel's surprise.

"Aqui?"

"Si. Aqui."

In a quarter hour he was face-up in a cool room, staring at a ceiling fan and itching to go for a stroll. It was late, but he was jazzed. He wanted a mojito, his first mojito, and a Cuba Libre to measure against the thousand rum and cokes he'd had before. Unafraid of empty streets, Sourdough suspected he was not the only one restlessly awake in a city so famous for high-energy.

On this suspicion, he was correct. There were others still up and about. Not a few blocks away, a nineteen year old girl was leaning against a pole, under a flickering light, making popping sounds with her chewing gum as she waited for her "uncle" to get off the public telephone.

Also awake, close to the Malecon, where the slapping of waves against concrete replaced the Son bands from earlier in the night, two men sipped warm rum, playing chess, too drunk and familiar to converse.

And on the other side of the city, humbly struggling out of a wheel-chair, onto a toilet seat, an underestimated man with a barrel of a chest, a gray beard, and too much pride to ring the bell for aid was kept awake by a new nightmare, the first fresh fear he'd felt in decades; one that seemed so unfathomable, his gut warned it was probably true.

There was also a ghost, and the ghost was quite drunk.

Aside from the apparition, they would all eventually sleep; none well.

Day 2

The smacking sun and noisy crowds and entitled turistas and accusing policia and rusting taxis with hissing drivers seemed all the same as every other day, dutifully filling their roles in painting a masterpiece atmosphere of veiled dangers and annoying rituals. Sandra navigated the landscape like a sailboat succumbing to the will of the ocean winds, on a course less the product of her calculations and more due to the encased Timex wristwatch she grasped in her left hand.

Lazaro did not give much direction, in his nature to expect her to remember past errands. Nothing substantially different now, a lazy Tuesday morning after a nothing Monday night. See what you can get for this watch, he suggested. No need for extended explanation. See what you can get for this watch.

Parque Central looked overcrowded, in the usual spackling way. The great statue of Marti, so impressive at night pointing East, spotlight shining up, flags on staffs like a circle of soldiers around. Not so impressive in the sunlight, it looked old. A wreath had been placed in the front, for any number of possible reasons, inviting the turistas as a photo op without much justification. Sandra did not wonder why he faced to the East, what he was pointing at, or the day's and wreath's significance. More important to find a buyer.

On the south side of the parque, men gathered in a circle, talking baseball, the Industrials, last night's loss in Cienfuegos, tomorrow's game at home. A famous hitter in a three-game slump, the consensus held that you are not a truly great player until you have worked through a truly unimpressive and exasperatingly long slump. With only pride invested in the team's success, hack analysis of every inning went on. Sandra could hear them from across the street, scanning for at least one who might want to know the time, and have a few pesos to exchange for a classy arm ornament.

Crossing to the parque took focus enough. After a wave of the old Chevrolet chariots swept past, she fell in with a crowd and held her look straight on. Most of the walkers were turistas; Sandra dared not glance in their eyes. Two policia stood with bad posture, pretending to hold the traffic at bay; she dared not check for their stares. A driver, leaning against his old Chevy, either out of fuel or taking another lazy break, hissed an invitation. And then she reached the parque sidewalk, and floated with some of the pedestrians toward the southern baseball circle.

See what you can get for this watch, he suggested. Lazaro meant one thing for certain—do not bring it back, but bring pesos instead. Sandra gripped the clear plastic case holding the item. It felt almost new, new enough, the watch was what mattered, and Lazaro had wisely set the time before giving it to her. He always thought of things like that, the little details important to customers, the little details that meant the difference between a "Yes" and a "No". But he never explained, or taught, so that all Sandra learned of business was that she would never be expected to be doing the thinking involved. Lazaro did not need an apprentice.

Getting paid was of utmost importance. The more wrists she looked at, the more opportunities she saw. But she had done this before, fenced items before, and knew enough not to be too aggressive. There were factors involved. Understood, unmentioned, implied factors. What mattered most was returning with pesos, a sufficient sum. Sandra wondered where the watch came from, casually acquired no doubt; from a friend of a friend who asked little in return, maybe a gift for a gesture as part of another transaction. Unimportant details. What mattered most was returning with pesos.

How many? Four would do. Unrealistic to expect more than four for a watch. And for a watch known stolen, shopped slyly on the street, a customer could bet squarely that an offer of three would not be turned away. Three pesos for a watch; that was a reasonable sale. Lazaro would not argue the point. He would nod, take the pesos, change the subject without note. Still, there were factors involved. There was the possibility three would be too few. How many did he expect?

She decided on the parque due to proximity. It was only a ten-minute walk from the apartment, and was populated with grand, thick trees providing welcome shade, and benches. He would not expect her back for a few hours, nothing doing mid-afternoon.

Only now she considered the negatives of the choice. Parque Central was indeed a grand place, very inviting for a number of reasons. Entirely bordered by streets, it was faced on three sides by high-end hotels. And this, mid-summer, meant the ever-present buzzing of digital cameras, jamble of foreign languages and ugly Spanish, and roaring engines and bellowing exhaust of the antique taxi cabs. Therefore, reconsidering as she sat on a concrete bench, more shade meant more people, more turistas unadapted to the sweltering Caribbean heat, and bringing with them, under the protective umbrella of the trees, more policia, as accusing and assuming as ever.

There were so many factors involved, she knew as she admired a genuine leather handbag, doted on the pale arm of a sophisticated-looking heiress on her way toward Habana Viejo. That arm held a watch of its own, a thin one with a golden band. An arm that never bought a watch for three pesos, Sandra mused. Her product was made for a man, of course, and the more she thought of it, the more she stared straight ahead at Marti's own hand, or at the concrete and flashing feet, the more she caught glimpses of pale wrists in the light, from the corner of her eye. Pale, bare wrists, the kind that could use a new watch. The kind willing to pay ten, twelve pesos for the novelty of the experience alone. Ten or twelve pesos, just for a watch. Ten or twelve pesos, just for the experience. This was no time to engage the thrill-seekers. This was no time for that kind of attention.

The process did not always run a straight line. Carry a watch to the parque, return with cash in its stead—this existed as only one of the possible equations. Mid-morning Sandra awoke on her own, unhurried, realizing she had spent the night, and Lazaro was out, likely out on the street. Though he never told her directly, she knew he loved the mornings. No matter how late the night went, he wasted no sunrise. A habit from the years of training, the early, dew-damped jogs and gym sessions. Those were the kinds of details he did mention, when he would finally settle down and kick back. The stories did not help him relax, but they made him feel young, and for sure that was what he preferred.

Now she felt tired again, only a few hours removed from her paltry night's rest. Her body anticipated the possibilities. The potential of the watch made her tense. It could serve as a needed time piece, money gladly and straightforwardly and painlessly exchanged. Or, it could serve as an excuse, for them. There are some who are particular of what they do and do not pay for. Then, a third scenario, it could serve as an excuse, for her. There are times, equally confounding, when it is easier to accept that you got a fair price for a Timex, or a better than fair price; that the possibility held of you being the one coming out ahead in the deal.

The Americano caught her off guard, approaching from behind with the boldness only a turista would even attempt.

"Excuse me, are you selling that watch?"

Later, Sandra would laugh when recalling how her first thought, void of emotion, was a simple "How young!" Knowing fully he had years on her—nine, a later revelation—the observation seemed absurd. But she was used to a certain kind of boy, not this kind, and she could think little else, since she had not understood what he asked.

"Perdon, senorita ... yo quiero comprar le watch, por favor."

What stood out the most were his eyes. They were big, brown, wide, and maybe it was unusual enough for a man not to wear sunglasses on this kind of bright day. The lashes stole the show, commanded the attention, decorated the ojos in such a magnetically charming fashion, Sandra could not look away, could not think about the question, could not answer it, and could not bring herself to act on the powerful impulse to retreat from the interaction rapidly.

He was the clean, daylight type, to be sure. She could sense from the hop in his step, the clothing—broken in sandals, designer-threaded cargo shorts, stylishly subtle, dirty t-shirt. A mini-backpack clung to one shoulder, colorful bracelets slipped around on his forearms, a pewter medallion on a chord around his neck. Relics she would later understand. Warnings she did not know to heed.

This dissected collision lasted less than a minute. He, double-checking a Spanish-English phrase book while she, scanning for the attention of the policia. A pair, in their bland gray attire, stood in crossed-arm conversation only meters away. She knew more than enough about male behavior to recognize machismo posturing. Was it on her account, or another's? Their calm surveying did not reveal. Some, identifying a possible infraction, would move to disrupt the situation immediately. Others, more seasoned and aware, would often let the scenario play itself further. Not out of a desire to accumulate evidence—none needed—but more as a consideration for the tourist, whose wallet may be scared shut upon realization of the power surrounding him. Ultimately, it was all a big transaction. In ways Lazaro would never feel compelled to explain.

In a flurry of action, she moved, her ultimate goal to be out of the situation, all previous and lesser agendas sacrificed to achieve that end state. With the handsome Americano mid-sentence into a repeat performance, Sandra handed him the encased Timex wristwatch, backing in retreat as she did, her eyes already checking for lanes out of the square, for pedestrians she might use as shields and obstacles against a policia pursuit, and with his bewildered and problematic reaction an unconsidered variable. She handed, backed away, turned, and kept moving, conscious of the volume of her shoe heels clacking against the concrete, and the burn in her thighs as she quickened the pace.

But Gabrel knew not to move on.

He pursued with a loud "Hey, wait! Perdon! Seniorita!" that broke into the sound of her shoes, and into the conversations about baseball nearby, and into the big dog posturing of the law, and the wreath in front of the statue was forgotten by the camera-toting Europeans, as a new subject of curiosity had appeared. The turistas watched the young man, his swift gait bounding across the parque. The locals knew enough to look forward, their eyes rotating in a triangular monitoring of the gringo, the girl, and the men with the guns, who were now also in rapid pursuit. In their faces an experienced reader could see self-ridicule over not being pro-active; now they would have to explain an "incident" on their watch. The story better end with a capture.

Sandra moved on adrenaline, slipping down an alley, into the first open door, unaware who she would find or what compensation they might insist on for the inconvenience and extensive danger of harboring her for the moment. She did not run, Sandra was not one to run, and would not in other circumstances have even feared the confrontation or legal ramifications. But on this day, Lazaro expected a profit. Now sans the product, she needed a new plan. It was for this that she moved with such purpose.

The Americano, having lost the trail, lost also the time to investigate, his mind quickly occupied instead with the presence of policia directly at his sides, though not directly looking at him. The proximics were uncomfortable, instincts slid the watch into his pocket, and with a feigned calm he swung abruptly, in fixed focus, toward the Capitolo just a few blocks away.

* * * *

Sandra kept a brisk pace as she maneuvered through Centro. The mid-afternoon arrived quickly, the hours she hoped to pass lazily after an effortless sale busy, instead, in active problem-solving. Avoiding the streets and corner bars where Lazaro often passed time, where his friends swatted flies and took note of familiar faces, she worked around, dipping down toward the Malecon. She kept one block inside, not wanting to be confused with the other, risk-taking walkers who dared the afternoon sun and offending the innocent families just out on the spot for a photo op. One block in, she kept a brisk pace, all the way to her abuelita's casa near the Universidad.

There, in a bedroom only ever used for sleeping, she had stored what she could. A few pesos, she was too embarrassed, there alone, to be curious of how few she had accumulated. But enough to buy a watch with. At least, enough to buy a watch from a girl in the parque. Her Abuelita was asleep in her armchair, the one piece of furniture bought new, long ago, so Sandra had been told. Perhaps that was why the old woman chose to sleep there more often than in the bed, acquired somehow along the way. Old crackers were spread on the table, these she took on her way out the door. Sandra hoped to really visit soon, for some talk; it had been a few weeks since she slept there.

Now returning, more straight arrow, the pesos tucked inside her skirt, she chose her route mostly thinking of the shade of the buildings on the narrower streets. Enough time, likely, for a nap. Sandra walked easier, lighter than before, knowing she would not need to fabricate a story or pass any sort of test. If she handed over the pesos without expression, then slunked down onto the bed and stared over at the wall, or up at the ceiling, as she usually did, there would not be questions. She liked to believe he chose not to ask as a courtesy, which had to at least be fractionally true. She would sleep a little, then maybe a change of clothes. She had not sweated much, but for variety's sake.

It was easy to rationalize the loss, as Sandra never had any good ideas of what she might spend her saved pesos toward. Abuelita did not accept gifts, her mind was too focused on giving away the possessions she might soon die owning. And there really was not anyone else she knew to buy for, who would not wonder, or ask, how she had managed the task. In fact, she thought, turning another block closer to Lazaro's place, today, with the young man, was the first time she had given anything away as a gift since the years, in the school, which seemed a bit less than real.

* * * *

These days, in Habana, life did not progress in the rapid, turbulent manner for which its reputation had been made. Storylines gradually built, characters slowly accepting their roles, plots seen through to culmination. But rarely with too much excitement, or too significant a climax, or too unpredictable a twist. These were days of consistency. And surely a person with years of upheaval behind them could appreciate, to some extent, knowing what lay soon ahead.

Much like the bigger picture of life, the days themselves slowly unwound. Perhaps because change is experienced on a personal level, and for so many citizens, working on the same floor of the same building, selling on the same section of the same calle, being scrutinized by the same uniformed policia for the same reasons, little change was noted. The most dramatic then—that of the rising and setting sun, shrunk in importance due to the absence of personal transition corresponding. True, most worked by day, slept by night, or vice versa. But with time and necessity and opportunity trumping rhythm, it could be said of an average Habana gentlemen a willingness to work at any hour, rest only when entirely necessary, and consider any course of action that included the rare potential of economic advancement. In other words, no edict or hard degree of law enforcement could entirely obliterate the human instinct to hustle. Especially with such an ever-inflating market of innocents idly inviting a quality scam.

So the midday passed into mid-afternoon, then as subtly into a hazy, warm night. The heat concentrated in the darkness, floating among the necks and the arms and the pale tourist legs until finding a pair to latch on to. Then the heat hung, like a cape, a weight not easily shrugged, though there were many distractions to fuel one onward, especially amid the saloons and restaurants frequented by the turistas. In Cuba there are two types of entrepreneurs—those who look at a building, estimating its market value, and those who look at the spaces and calles in between, the paths traversed between hotspots recommended in thick, fraying paperback travel books.

To invest in a building means to take on a partner; a large, not always silent, fifty-one-percent-ownership partner. But forty-nine of something is more than ninety-percent of nothing. There were many who longed for such adequate stability. And they stood on this night, behind wood-paneled bars, or at entrances, holding menus, offering deals and welcoming expressions, wearing black and white waiter outfits, scanning passersby for interested eye-contact. Being careful not to harass.

But in the sporadically lit city, especially the outskirts of the Viejo district, on into Centro, a pedestrian passed in and out of darkness along most routes. And in the black spots shadows lurked, loitering an offense only rarely enforced, whispering quickly, joining pace for a few steps, offering their moment-long pitch. Their eyes keenly monitoring the uniforms; their thoughts constantly reminding them of the treasure-trove market worth every bit of this risk.

Sandra woke from her nap expecting to put on her blue top, the spaghetti-strap, bare-shoulders one, to go with the silver shoes, which she preferred more for their sturdy, thick heel and decent cushioning than their looks. She woke expecting to meet Lazaro by the public telephones along Calle Zapata, instead finding him standing by the bed, smoking a cigarette and watching her lie under the thin white sheet.

"Good news. An old friend of mine has returned. You will meet him tonight. An old friend."

Sandra did not reply, nor allow an expression to cross her face. She held nothing back, but simply had no emotion to show. Besides, this was not a conversation.

"He is French. I met him years ago, when I used to still work at the gym. The French man has been back three times since then. He works in some kind of business. Some kind of trading."

Sandra lifted her torso, supporting herself on her left elbow and forearm, watching Lazaro smoke. Unlike many Cubanos, he did not smoke all the time, or when he could afford to, or when he could borrow one from a friend or passerby. Lazaro smoked when he had something on his mind, or after a good meal.

"Did you eat something?"

"No. I think we will all have dinner tonight. Are you hungry now?"

"No."

"We will go to a place nearby. When he calls, I will tell him. The French man is familiar with the area. He can meet us there. You should wear the red top, maybe with the white skirt."

Sandra reclined again, closing her eyes. Lazaro flicked the last ash of the cigarette away, and moved to the other room.

* * * *

The wide-bladed, powerful ceiling fan whirled steadily, silent under the hum of the air conditioning box jammed through the window by the door. Between the two efforts, the small room with attached shower and sink held a deliciously frigid temperature. Gabrel lay spread eagle, naked except for the medallion around his neck, face-up on the spacious, springy bed, basking in the chill, feet slightly propped on a pillow. It had been a tiring two days.

The trip from Los Angeles began in the late afternoon yesterday, through the airline's international hub in Phoenix to a long layover in Mexico City. Flights from there to Habana were frequent, easily done when timed well, but he'd gone for a deal on a website, and used the time practicing the Spanish tongue. When he finally cleared customs and found a trustworthy cab driver, then been led to the city center and dumped at the man's friend's casa particular, he was too hungry for breakfast and too thrilled to have arrived to acknowledge his state of fatigue.

Maybe that explained why so many details from this inaugural day still seemed a tad off-kilter. The Americano maintained a habit, a ritual, when arriving in a new place. Soaking in the faces and facades and atmosphere, he would walk and walk and walk, ignoring street names on the initial go-round, mapping the lay of the city in his mind. The guidebook he carried, often tucked away in the small black bag on his back, served only to inform on specific locations and their significance. He did not utilize the many maps intermixed. Due to his lack of a natural compass, this often meant backtracking, making up for wrong turns, and passing the same landmarks multiple times toward the end of the day, when he elected to return to the casa. For a city on an island, with an obvious body of water to the North and the sun to assist from there, the effort had been frustratingly mistake-filled. Lying on the bed, bathing in the chill, he could attribute the judgment lapses to a jet-lagged brain. At least for the first half-day.

After the odd event in the parque, from which he walked off wearing the cheaper-than-it-had-looked Timex strapped onto his wrist, Gabrel found the Capitolo inexplicably closed, and a few minutes later, recognizing the fringe details of the edge of a tourist sector, he sunk onto a stool in the Bar Monserrate, ordering the first of several mojitos. The guidebook recommended this choice, a beverage he'd never downed before, and the mint and the sugar and the lime mixed with rum refreshed him as much as it hazed things. Natural drinkers must be careful not to dive in too early, but then, he remembered remembering, this was Ernest's old stomping ground. There were legends about, and the implication was clear.

He ordered only having to repeat "Yo quiero un mojito por favor" once, the first tall narrow glass emptied quickly on the adrenaline of making the grade. From there he continued as any reasonable being might, seeing no reason to find a new stool in a new bar with a less understanding waiter when here, now on, he could just say, "Un otro."

The drying coolness sobered him, too. It felt very important that he not fall asleep; very important the envelope be pushed. Buzzed exhaustion had not worked so well in the swelter of mid-afternoon. But now showered, not resting but conscious, now cool, he knew he would head out again. This time for the nightlife, with abandon he would fall into it, let suggestions and instincts guide the way. He knew to expect bad intentions. He knew not to trust right away. He knew he would be surprised, maybe disappointed, but that the night would not work out as he expected, never did, so no point carrying any anticipation out the door with him.

What he did not know was how uncomfortable it could feel, or how deviant those bad intentions could be. Lying under the fan, goose bumps on naked skin suggesting the time had come to rise, he did not have a hint what he was not prepared for.

※ ※ ※ ※

Fernando Rodriguez shuffled slowly around the room, using his bare feet to kick clothes and papers out of the way as he continued the search for his loafers. It was the middle of the week, a night he would gladly spend listening to the radio, not just loaferless but half-naked. There was still enough rum in last night's bottle—positioned capless where they left it, out on the counter by the kitchen sink. There was no need to walk across town.

Raul called at ten in the morning, trying not to sound agitated. Fernando was still in his bed, and it seemed the two had just spoke; Raul had stumbled home only a few hours before. If he had forgotten his wallet, something like that, he would have casually returned for it later. A call, so early, was most out of the ordinary.

"The cantina tonight, ten o'clock, can you be there?"

"Why would I want to go there?"

"Can you be at the cantina?"

"Why don't you just come here?"

"Ten o'clock. Pick a table. I'll be a little late. Walk safely, amigo."

"Why should I be there at ten if you're gonna be-"

Raul had hung up the phone, effectively ruining an already unpromising day. Now Fernando sifted through the mess of his home, finding the lost shoes in two different rooms, and re-channeling his focus to locating a clean collared shirt.

To meet two nights in a row—and publicly, no less. Fernando chuckled as he guessed what his handlers would think of it. He should put a few lines in the next report, out of nowhere, non-sequitor style: "Attended Memorial Parade 13 July, no VIPs present. Observed four black SUVs traveling in formation morning of 15 July, stopping at Treasury Office on Calle 14, no VIPs identified. Invited Cuban agent to house for chess, rum drink, and porno watching night of 16 July. Met with contacts in Agriculture Department …"

Yes, that would get their assholes pretty tight, Fernando thought, grinning as he buttoned up the shirt. By the time he finished the task, his grin was gone. The assholes. They probably did not even read his reports any more. He had not received last month's pay, and when he sent a complaint, he received no reply to that. This month's sum should arrive tomorrow, and it was possible he would receive two months' worth at once. "Possible, but not very goddamn likely" he thought, heading for the door. If he did not get paid tomorrow, if the money did not come ... well, what would he do? What could he do?

Fernando sighed, turning toward Habana Centro and stepping out his stride. Why didn't Raul just drop by?

*   *   *   *

Fernando always assumed that when the day finally came, and all the cards were laid face-up on the table of truth, revelations about his performance would likely pale in comparison to the actions of others. What others, he could not say. Which actions, he could only guess. It was a world of guesses, misinterpretations, high-stakes gambling and now, it seemed, forgotten pieces on a forgotten chess board.

Fernando was only a young teen when the Revolution changed his world. He remembered how dirty they all looked in the parades, how excited everyone seemed, how busy his father's restaurant was, in those early days of mass jubilation. There was little time for school work, no time for friends, as washing dishes, taking orders, and restocking the cook's supplies were the top priority. Everything happened so fast, allegiances demonstrated so boldly by so many, it was at least understandable that Fernando did not notice, in those times, his Father's solemn face, his silence, surrounded and invisible among a sea of voices repeating propaganda slogans with such conviction, you would think they had thought up the catchy phrases themselves.

The various shades of reality revealed themselves to Fernando one at a time, a year at a time. He remembered, at sixteen, listening to the radio, his father in the kitchen, washing the dishes, his attention loyal to the tedious task, reports of the American embargo, Fernando understanding the position of Cuba in the world with such eye-opening awe.

He remembered at seventeen, thinking nothing of the newly-locked storage room in the back of the restaurant, not until the day they came, demanded it be unlocked, he alone on the property, without a key, them smashing the lock with the butt of a sturdy, clean rifle, and them finding nothing, nothing at all but a perfectly empty room, inexplicably locked. Fernando remembered the little man in the suit, his expressionless face, peering in only for a moment before going back to his car, no sign of surprise, the driver speeding away. Later that night, after the soldiers had gone, before they would come back and permanently, forever, close the restaurant, Fernando remembered returning to the closet, barely big enough for a few barrels, and finding a silk beige envelope on the ground, a dark stain soaked well into half of it.

He remembered at eighteen, waking in the early hours to the sound of the knock, finding his mother awake, as if waiting for them, finding his father gone, his mother and the soldiers both far less surprised than he.

Those events seemed so deeply buried in the recesses of his mind, he almost regretted never writing them down, or not writing them down as they progressed. His father's unscheduled returns, which his mother always seemed to know were imminent; twice in a month, then twice in a week, then not for half a year—sporadic, consistently under the veil of the dark nights, but otherwise not tied to anything Fernando could quite put his finger on.

One night Fernando went to sleep, a grown man with a wife, a home, a good enough job driving taxi around the city, and a mother downstairs, gazing out at the children playing in the calle as the sun slowly started to set. Before he opened his eyes, he knew in his heart that the powerful hand over his mouth belonged to his father, and that this was the moment of clarity he'd been longing for.

Fernando swung around a last corner and stopped, the cantina on the other side of the street, with a handful of locals in the middle of dinner. He checked his wristwatch: nine-fifty-two. He entered without a gesture to the waiter, or acknowledgement of the outstretched menu, moving to a table by the wall with clear vision of the entrance as well as the door to the restroom, and the passage behind the bar, into the kitchen. Damn Raul, had him on his toes, sweating and needing a drink, and it better be for a good reason, he thought. But good reasons were not in abundance these days.

He took another broad survey of his fellow patrons. This was a local joint, the kind of place with good enough food to enjoy yourself, but not marketing to the turistas who might wander this way. Fernando ordered a rum on ice and thought it through some more. A clever choice on Raul's part. Fernando had been here before, used to stop by often, years ago. Though never with Raul. Those were the days before the arrangement. Either Raul was in a gaming mood this evening, or he was trying to make a point. Fernando's curiosity was peaked. The rum came and he sipped leisurely, wanting it to last, and not wanting to dull his faculties yet.

Raul arrived just before midnight, Fernando well into his third round of the cheapest, clearest bottle from behind the bar. By now his thoughts had drifted through so many different possibilities, and beyond the current meeting, to fantasies involving the waitresses, and theories for fixing the black outs, he had nearly forgotten who he waited for. Seeing Raul approach, unsteady, eyes darting about, trying to control his breathing as if he'd been doing some running, Fernando decided not to begin on the attack. This was Raul's idea. Let him throw the first pitch.

Raul nodded, sat down opposite, then ordered a drink of his own. He smoked a cigarette as he entered, but now crushed it out, finished, and dug through his shirt pocket for the box, and another. Fernando had chosen the more powerful seat, and could sense Raul's nervousness, his back to everything, his options for avoiding eye contact very few. When the drink arrived, and he took a fair swig, he finally looked up, leaning forward.

"Do you have anything you wish to say to me, Fernando?"

Fernando laughed, leaning back. He did not appreciate how nervous he was becoming, on account of Raul. In situations like this, he recalled, when you have more questions than answers, stay calm, say little. The answers cannot hide forever.

"A silly question, my friend, you are the one who suggested-"

"On this occasion, Fernando, do not call me your friend. I think it is in the best interest of our friendship, on this occasion, if we act as professionals." Raul took another big drink, pushing the glass away as he swallowed, suddenly reminded of a need for sobriety. He stared at Fernando, and the stare was returned. He leaned forward again, his voice hushed, and of an honest, somber tone.

"I was summoned to a meeting today."

A pause. Thinking. "So?"

"Do you have any idea how long it has been since I was summoned to a meeting? Do you have any idea? Fifteen years, Fernando! Fifteen years!"

The revelation was startling. Fernando, himself, had never been summoned to a meeting, not since the first day. But his situation was very different—he was the outsider, the forward deployed. It was understood that his correspondence with Higher would be long-distance and not of any regular pattern, great caution taken to protect such a fragile operation. But Raul's situation, the limited amount Fernando knew of it, was much different. Maybe he did not know, Fernando realized. Maybe he just always assumed.

"Last night, an arrival." Raul was on his third cigarette now.

"What do you mean?"

"There is a new man, Fernando," Raul leaned forward, his eyes fierce in the night's odd lighting. "I have a new assignment."

"A turista?"

"That, old friend, is what I was hoping you could tell me."

The waiter had returned, stood beside the table now. How long he'd been standing there, neither was sure. It was getting late, this was not a late night establishment, it was the middle of the week, and the two of them, the lone patrons remaining, were equally dry of rum.

"Un otro, senor?"

"Si, claro."

"Y tu, senor?"

"Si, si. Gracias."

The mesero walked off, and Raul leaned back, watching Fernando's expressions. He could see, as small understandings built into grand realizations, with their desperate ramifications, Fernando's eyes widen, his Adam's Apple rise and fall, a lone vein near his left temple throb awake. Now it was Fernando who leaned forward, whose tone carried considerable gravity, and whose clenched fist left sweaty residue on the table where it lay.

"Who is he?"

"He is an American."

"But there are many Americans here."

"Not like this one, I am told."

"What do you know of him?"

"That he is my new assignment. That it is of the highest priority. That I will report daily, and must be prepared to be contacted for updates at any time."

Fernando shuffled his feet. They had never had a conversation like this, between them. These waters were deep, and dangerous. If Raul was telling the truth, it meant that the Cuban government believed a new American agent had recently arrived and was operating on the island. There had not been "fresh meat", to Fernando's knowledge, in two decades.

The timing held a level of possibility to it. But that could also just prove Commandante Barbuda had not lost the faculty of paranoia. Then there was that other timing coincidence. Fernando had not been paid, or received any response to reports and requests, in two months. He could see Raul was expecting a reply. He wanted to ask if they knew about his pay.

Instead of asking, he chuckled, thanking the waiter as the fresh drinks arrived. "So, if you have this promotion," Fernando took a sip, "who will be now working on me?"

Raul let his glass sit, standing, pulling out some cash, and tossing it down for the bill. "I don't know. They did not say. They did not mention you once, the whole time. Good night, Fernando." The older man turned to go, a bit of a slump in his posture, much less rushed or concerned than he was coming in. Fernando watched, and suddenly felt like spiders were crawling from the glass, up his arm. The information was too rapid, the situation too delicate to garner a quality reaction.

He stayed in his seat, alone, another forty minutes, the staff cleaning and closing politely around him, letting him finish both drinks and stumble out at his own pace. "Nice place," Fernando thought, reaching for tables and chairs to assist his escape. "I should find more excuses to come here."

✳   ✳   ✳   ✳

Only a few blocks away, Gabrel was quickly coming around to the idea he had walked into the wrong place. He'd rested, lingered longer in his room than originally planned, his mind going back and forth on when to go out, how long to stay out. If he hit the streets at nine, and was drinking at around the same rate as the afternoon's performance, he would be passed out by one, somewhere. That would be an even earlier exit from the scene than on arrival the night before, and Sourdough was very confident, last night, there were happenings around town. Some cultures have vibrant nightlife, the kind that spills out into the street, as if fueled by moonlight. Others, like this one, Sourdough figured, were not of the nature to be so outgoing. Whether due to modesty, humility or necessity, Habana kept itself behind closed doors. Gabrel could only hope those doors opened at the sound of a turista's knock.

During the daylight, struggling though he did with navigation, he'd become comfortable with a route, a right turn exiting the casa particular, two blocks, past the corner, open-air bar, hang a left, and then straight down an alley that was running behind the Capitolo, and would continue straight through to the Parque Central, the Marti statue, the place where he had acquired the watch, where grand hotels stood guard and policia, too. This alley seemed a good place to start the evening, lined with small stores and street food toasted on portable, rolling grills. Gabrel noticed the monetary exchange was mostly pesos here, not the new, official bills. That meant the food was for locals. Just what he was hungry for.

The walk down the alley to the parque felt longer in the dark. Many faces watching, saying nothing. Policia, in their light brown shirts, dark brown pants, distributed at road intersections in pairs, watching, saying nothing. When he finally reached the bright lights and high-end patio cafes with pale-skinned patrons calculating tips, he made the decision to swing back around, find a joint in the shadows, and walk in like he owned the place—eyes straight ahead, just above the returning stares, all the way to the bar.

And this he did, finding himself squeezed awkwardly on a stool with a bad leg, more work to try to sit on it than stand beside, but no room beside, with a wild-looking fellow in a Red Sox t-shirt virtually spitting every word of English he could remember at Sourdough, and the gentleman's lady friend, all smiles, no English, progressively moving in on his space from the right.

"Hey, whe' you from? Whe' you come from? American, ye'? Whe' you from?"

The television set, clamped to a mantle above the center of the bar, was showing music videos. One out of every three was a Shakira song, a fact nobody seemed to mind, her body gyrating to a rhythm Gabrel knew he would never totally feel. That was real culture—your body's reaction to a beat. That was one of those things that defined you; beyond your powers of decision.

Gabrel had ordered a mojito, and hardly finished saying the word before understanding that this was not the kind of place where you walked in and ordered a mojito. The beverage of choice was beer from a can, with a few drinking straight, clear rum, sipping it from glasses. The bartender first rummaged for some usable mint, poured and mashed the lime juice and sugar haphazardly, quickly mixing the soda water and rum with a look of near inconvenience that yet another lost turista had entered his lair. Where the other customers either ignored Gabrel or eyed him as an opportunity, the bartender did not seem amused. To him, Sourdough meant nothing, or trouble, and pay for a couple mojitos was not worth the greater gamble. But he did not know how to say it in English, so he just turned back to the videos on the set, and hoped the young man would finish and go and not order one more.

Instincts and buzz both spirited him toward the door, and for better or worse, Gabrel went back into the night.

* * * *

Sandra rested her head on her hand, elbow sturdy on the restaurant table, her other hand playing with the fork she had used to clean off the plate. She read once, in a magazine, of the things some girls do to maintain firm bodies. Forced vomiting, or smoking cigarettes to curb appetites, or mind tricks to block out the hunger. It was possible some of the girls she knew employed these or similar tactics—especially the older ones, who more often seemed self-conscience of their fit in their clothes. Sandra knew, she just knew, this would never be her. It was the kind of subject that only occurred to her after finishing a big meal, and only in a casual way. She loved the taste of a good bistek, or pasta, and on that rarest occasion, fried or broiled shrimp on angel hair, maybe with a thick white sauce mixed in.

It was also only after the meal when she always made the mental note to mention to Lazaro, maybe tomorrow, that this pasta mix was her most favorite dish. He was always the one who ordered—or moreso, made suggestions of what should be ordered for her, adjusting her "favorite" to whatever the gentleman seemed most inclined to want to hear. And his guesses brought slimy grins of approval. Lazaro always knew what to say. Maybe, she thought, that was why she never mentioned it. Maybe he knew better than she did what she might enjoy.

The Frenchman sat between them, still working on his meal. He and Lazaro had been flying through a conversation with a lot of laughter and storytelling since they met at the place an hour ago. Sandra remembered to look back at him every time he looked at her. Aside from that duty, she did not speak English or French—their talk seemed filled with familiar sounds of both—so she ate undisturbed, and relaxed.

Sandra guessed that he was about forty. From the way they conversed, an outsider might think he and Lazaro shared a long history. She knew this was not necessarily true. Lazaro had a way of warming to people, men and women, of making them feel at ease, comfortable, and familiar. It was possible they had only met one other time, a business trip when the man had been lucky enough to be spotted, approached, and introduced to the world of pleasure and ease that only a seasoned, smart Cubano like Lazaro could provide. Lazaro knew everyone worth knowing, had done everything you would like to, knew the easiest way into and out of every situation a man might accidentally become entangled in on a visit to the island. Watching him now dominate the conversation, his pencil-thin arms jabbing out in front of him—no doubt another Olympic boxing story—Sandra felt the safety of association. That was Lazaro, and she was with him.

For his part, the Frenchman was typical. He sat with bad posture, hunched over his plate, sometimes speaking with his mouth full of food, the way a man might behave in his home, but only a man of notable confidence might behave in public. In the slumped formation, his paunch was exaggerated. He did not look the type to worry much about his appearance, he did not look the type too self-conscious. With nothing to do but rotate her gaze from the empty plate, to Lazaro, to him, Sandra chose not to wonder too much what they sat laughing about. It was a good, satisfying meal. That was plenty to consider for now.

* * * *

Gabrel rested on the stool, smoking the cigarette, studying his reflection in the long mirror that stretched the length of the back of the bar. His nose and eyes appeared quite skewed, and there were a number of possibilities to consider before assigning blame to either the age and weathering of the mirror or his diminishing powers of perception. The bartender had given the cigarette, he could see the back of the black man's bald head in the reflection, too, standing on the far end, chatting with the only other customer, a local buddy, and trying to not be too nervous. There was another person present, a woman sitting two stools to Gabrel's left. But she did not count as a customer. She was a solicitor.

They were waiting on a can of Coca-Cola, to complete the rum and coke Sourdough had ordered. On the walk from the last establishment, he found himself drifting down his only known route, back toward the casa particular, and summoned the strength to fight that instinct, stop at a bar and order a can of cheap beer. It was cold, and surprisingly good following the mojito. The crisp taste stroked his ego, and before it was gone, a block later, he was sitting at another bar, the open air one built into the corner, where he needed to turn to finish the trip. It was a good place to stop—hard to get lost from here, no matter how drunk he became. And equally inviting in how empty, and chill, and Cuban it seemed, open in the name of being open, by no means out of popular demand.

The bartender's age—ancient—also argued for a stop. He had a small frame, and a disarming smile. No question he had stories to tell—a good challenge for Gabrel's Spanish studies.

But they did not get far into the talk. Gabrel asked for a rum and coke. The bartender had the rum, but not the other. Gabrel, having placed a large bill on the counter, looked trusting enough, and the bartender picked up the bill, handed it to one of the two other patrons, barked some orders, and the man was off. A few minutes later he returned, but with an actual Coca-Cola. The Spanish flew fast between them, and with a heavy accent Gabrel had no familiarity with, but he understood enough from the gestures and actions that it was economically foolish to use actual Coke in a mixed drink, when the cheaper cola was available. So the man had been sent off again, and they continued to wait, going on fifteen minutes, Gabrel smoking the second apologetically-offered cigarette.

As time past, the matter's complexity multiplied. Gabrel began to wonder if he had fallen for an old game—the bill he gave them could buy twenty Cuba Libres, and a place like this, off the beaten path, out of the turista section by a few blocks, and therefore outside of the policia focus, might be able to get away with something like this, so late in the night, dealing with a young man who probably did not possess the linguistic skills or legal knowledge to pursue his being wronged. As Gabrel thought it through, his eyes and nervous looks out into the darkness of the alley, where the errand boy was last seen, gave him away.

The bartender worried, too. As it were, this was not a plan of that kind. He had gone a long time without any incidents, and was beginning to regret the whole scenario, second-guessing his enthusiasm when the boy first walked up and sat down. He did not have even the money with him to reimburse, if the jackass he sent on the errand decided not to return. He had thought about closing down an hour ago, and stayed open only so his friends could continue their talk of the Industrials. He, too, was feeling suckered.

But the bartender's anxiety, and Gabrel's paranoia, were of little rank compared to the woman's fear. She had seen the young man arrive, seen him finish his beer with the zest of a pirate on a binge, seen him not look away when she carried her smile toward him, took the seat and convinced him to buy her a drink. Now, her own beer nearly done, she hesitated to push conversation, afraid saying the wrong thing just might scare him away. He was worried about his money. He was going to leave. It was late, and she needed this, mostly because she had no expectations of a good night, and then suddenly enormous, fantastic hopes, hopes that now hung in front of her face, unignorable. She was too old, and too aware, to let such strings be pulled. Such situations—so extremely bad or extremely good with no middle ground—were not very healthy for her head.

* * * *

Lazaro had left them an hour ago. He was probably over at the hotel, or Pablo's, or just out front on the concrete steps. He was probably smoking, Sandra thought, planning or revising tomorrow's agenda. Besides, the Frenchman bought him a pack on their way to the room. Might as well put it to use.

They shared a bottle of wine with the meal, a sweet taste Sandra was not so used to, and now she could feel its fatigue, pulling her eyelids closed. She thought about letting them fall, but could not be certain the Frenchman was completely passed out. His right hand, tan and thick and showing off a fat gold ring, rested on her belly, he face down next to her, Sandra staring up at the cracks and chipped away paint on the ceiling. Every minute or two the hand moved, gliding a few centimeters toward her bare breasts, or a few centimeters below her bare belly. Aside from this action, no reason to suspect another round. But always better to weigh on the side of caution. Better to still be awake when Lazaro quietly returned, than to not.

It was possible he wouldn't. Not until morning. Sandra wondered how long the Frenchman would be in town, and why, when seemingly so familiar with the workings of the city, and certain places, he had not managed to learn any Spanish. Often, the Europeans could speak it, or at least variations on Italian or Portuguese that sufficiently communicated the main idea. She wondered why paint had been chipped from the ceiling. She wondered how old that room was. Maybe he could speak Spanish, and chose, with Lazaro, to keep her out of the conversation. He had not said a word to her, even once they were alone; only a few murmurs in French, and the kind that was more talking to himself—or to nobody in particular.

Sandra suddenly realized she'd let her eyes shut. The Frenchman's heavy hand slid again, ever slightly. Maybe he would even like it; sometimes they found satisfaction in watching her sleep. She always felt more comfortable on her side, but stayed on her back for the night. Lazaro would return before sunrise. He would want to escort his friend out of the Centro, at least out of this particular section of it. That would be the decent thing to do—to shield their guest from those who might try to take advantage.

* * * *

Everything was blurry, but in a way that Gabrel knew if he just reached out, grabbed hold of something, grabbed hold very tight, the situation was still salvageable. Events unfolded rapidly, first the almost surprising return of the man, with the cheaper cola and relatively correct change. This breathed new life into everyone's ambitions, the bartender then generously—perhaps connivingly—pouring two drops of rum for each drop of cola into the glass, stirred and sent straight away down Gabrel's throat. Gulp by gulp, the night grew more agreeable. Soon she was sitting very close, their knees and thighs brushing against one another as they sat on the stools, the bartender keeping a respectful distance at first, on the far end in conversation, sending an encouraging smile and nod toward Sourdough every few minutes. Then, he was in front of them, she whispering in his left ear the activities they could begin as soon as he liked, the bartender complimenting the cause in his right ear, with colorful words of recommendation, guaranteeing the experience well worth Gabrel's time.

Then they were gone, turning the corner, Sourdough realizing in a moment of clarity that if they continued a mere few blocks he would be back in the air-conditioned room of the casa. Instead, a quick right turn, into an alley so dark he nearly lost sight of the aged, worn body of the woman—did she say her name was Ana?—who pulled him through an opening in a long wall, a place a door should be, into the guts of a building's first floor, toward a room that looked like it was once meant to be a storage closet. She knocked, then again, holding tight to his hand, remembering to periodically stroke his forearm, and it was all so very, very dark—did she say her name was Ana? Something about being a Fidelista? Was that something he'd asked her? That sounded like something he'd ask.

A thin, shirtless man who had clearly been asleep opened the door, and quick, uncatchable words were exchanged. The man reached back into his room for a cigarette, then turned on a light—the sole star in this galaxy, Sourdough thought. Nodding to Gabrel, he left. Then they were inside. Then they were alone. And in the bright, tiny room, as she sat down on the bed, anxiously removed her top, revealing the raw facts of her age and wear, pleading for pesos as she worked down his shorts, he thought that if he could just reach out, grab a firm hold of something and hang on, the clarity might return.

He did, and it did, and there was no way, simply no way this was going to happen. He had another twenty bill in his pocket, likely more than she would ask for. Lifting her hand away from him, he gave her the paper cash. Pulling his shorts back on, he could see she was starting to cry. It was an unwinnable, entirely unsalvageable situation, the kind a guy with a working brain would know how to sidestep. All Gabrel knew how to do, now, was get out, and he did not take the time to be careful, or nod to the man waiting outside the door, or do anything other than stumble pathetically, back the route they had come, down toward his lodging, and into his room. He had not remembered to turn off the air-conditioning, and the chilling contrast from the night's thick heat, the added sweat brought on by the awkward, rough situation, was a punch that he gladly took on. As only a drunk can, he stripped down, and showered, and crawled into bed. The shower did little to help.

* * * *

"You are losing your ability to recognize your own paranoia."
"You've been wrong about that before."
"Sooner or later, I won't be wrong anymore."
"Not yet."
"You'll be wrong about that someday, too. Sooner or later, you'll be wrong about that."

Comandante Barbuda reached up, turning off the lamp just above the bed. The fixture used to be over on the side, on the small table, but they had readjusted it, redone the wiring and everything, to make it easier to reach up, turn it off. Sometimes, before the change, he would go to sleep without reading anything at all. It was an unsettling behavior, and he'd begun to worry he was losing his edge. The nighttime was a good time to re-read the important stories of the day, refresh on them before a night that might expose new angles, bring forth new revelations, to be acted on the next morning. Finished now with a newspaper from London, he did not turn off the light to sleep, but to see better out the open window, the city lights, and the parts of the city without any light at all. Barbuda sighed. He wished he were alone.

"Maybe they are just guessing."

"So, you are coming around to the possibility that they *are* doing maneuvers."

"I wouldn't call them maneuvers. Blind stabs."

"The timing is too coincidental."

"It's been coincidental before. And to be frank, maybe this is too predictable."

"You're not much help."

"I've no intention to be, Comandante."

Barbuda breathed in deeply, trying to sit up in the bed as straight as possible, rolling his shoulders back, filling his puffed out chest with air, and then exhaling. Breathing had become a scheduled exercise event. But at least he was still alive.

Focusing on the positives had gotten him through worse lots before, and would do so again. For the most part, he was limited to the bed until morning, when strong, careful arms would reposition him in the chair, and push him, and as much dignity as he could fit into the sweat suit, wherever he pointed to go. Likely only to the window, to water the plants, and of course for a bath and more time on the toilet than he needed to read the whole Economist. But he was still reading, and writing, and planning. Bold plans, the only kind he chose to entertain. Tonight, once again, he worried over them, and fresh, threatening enemy maneuvers.

"It must be paranoia, and its your own fault. Who else knows the plan?"

"No one but you."

"Of course. You create these mathematical equations yourself, then you marvel at how they compute. Paranoia, Comandante. Without any method for discovering your intentions, they are forced to react blindly. If they knew even the smallest detail, something insignificant, but something they could be unquestionably certain of, they would have the option of staying the course, or awaiting the move. You are secretive to a negative degree. Your perfect deception challenges their manhood. It forces them to be bold."

"We've always prevailed in the past."

"You've never aspired this way. You are baiting the marlin too cock-sure of yourself."

Perhaps, Barbuda considered. It was a valid point, at least, that he'd given them no choice but maneuvers. It would still help to know their intent. They were not the kind to train variably; if there was a mission, it was a clearly defined concept, with a clearly defined purpose and clearly defined end state for success.

"Do you think they take advice from drunk ghosts?"

"If they did, they'd have bested you a long while ago."

"How can they possibly think any gain, after all this time, could be considered victory for them?"

"That's the point of discussion, isn't it? Who is after what gain, at this point? What angles are completely exhausted, what points are entirely won or hopelessly lost? Who is after what?"

"I know what I'm after."

"And you think they've guessed it?"

"We'll find out."

"Going on the counter could stoke a lot of fire from ash."

"We are still in the stronger position. We still hold the advantages."

"We? And what of you?"

"Not a worry of yours, drunk. I am going to rest now. I don't want you planting bad seeds."

Comandante wiggled his body down, into the soft bedding. The drunken ghost's comments held as much truth as his own. It was an odd race, especially now, having evolved into such a complex web of guessing, posturing, and unnoticed missteps. But he knew he still held the advantage. What could they possibly hope to achieve?

Of course, he knew the answer to that question, too. The bastards just wanted the last strike. He had pummeled them so thoroughly, he would continue to pummel them. So even if they got that last, paltry move, to what end?

Day 3

Gabrel rose early, despite his condition when retiring, only a few hours before. This was a habit of his, in a strange place. It had nothing to do with a heightened sense of alarm, or fear, or a night-before-Christmas eagerness. But it was an undeniable restlessness, and it was just as well. There was little in the rented room but four walls of enclosed comfort. He was not yet so old that vacations were an exercise in relaxation.

Sourdough had been surprised, that first night, at the sticker in the window that authorized the taxi's destination as an official casa particular. He expected—maybe hoped for—an off the record place. Now walking toward Habana Viejo, again taking note of the very visible police presence, Gabrel was beginning to realize the reality of the rumors. Before he could receive the key on that first night, standing in the living room of the house, the smiling, Spanish-speaking gentleman with the carefully trimmed mustache and blue tank top meticulously inspecting his passport, writing down the full name, the full passport number in a well-kept ledger, Sourdough wondered why such fuss at such a late hour. Leafing through his guidebook the next day, in the morning, he stumbled across a small blurb explaining the casa particular requirement of submitting the names of guests within twenty-four hours, or risk losing their license to host. Funny, to imagine a little fat man in a tiny, steaming office, sweat dripping from his bald head onto pages and pages of names and locations across the island, he trying in vain to keep a map as up to date with push pins as possible, for fear of inspection. Sourdough ... where is Sourdough? Ah, Habana Centro, put the push pin

THERE. Good, now to lunch. An amusing image, as Gabrel continued his morning trek.

He was walking to Habana Viejo—today hoping to get the tourist landmarks out of the way, and ideally spend time in the Museo de la Revolucion. It was always better to study the big picture, then dig into the details. And in this instance, there were two views on the "Big Picture"—there was the view he had grown up learning, and there was the view he had only glimpses of, in books and on internet sites. The perspective would be clear in the museum—it would be presented exactly as they wanted it. Making his way East, noticing the ugly black exhaust pouring out of the vintage cars, Gabrel could not help wonder if a third position existed, waiting to be revealed.

∗ ∗ ∗ ∗

Raul was awake early, too. He could feel the butterflies in his stomach as he approached the office of tourism. Would they know to expect him? Would they question his credentials? It had been a long time. Would there be any familiar faces? The office was scheduled to open at eight o'clock. Raul glanced at his watch: seven-thirty. Squinting through the closed blinds, he could not see anyone moving inside. Slipping the narrow, steel tools from his pocket, he moved to the front door. A man of his position did not need to wait for common employees. They would not dare ask for credentials.

Inside, the layout of the office had not changed much in the last decade. The same number of desks, the same cubicle positioning, the coffee maker on the same counter, even looked the same model. Where once were only typewriters now there were computers—Raul had no experience with those, and feared the information may no longer be kept in the filing cabinets, but in some sort of electronic database. He decided to sit down, wait, and jump all over the first sorry employee to walk through the door. Whoever they were, they were going to get him the information he wanted. A man of his position did not need to dirty his fingers in filing cabinets, anyway. Raul sat down in the receptionist's chair, propping his feet on the desk, and remembering the 1980's.

∗ ∗ ∗ ∗

Fernando opened his eyes, and groaned. He'd passed out on his own front porch, not even enough awareness to make it through the door and plop down on the bed. The uneven boards and occasional poking-out nail had been a pain all night, a massage gone wrong, and he would pay for it dearly today. The sun was well into the sky—it was probably almost ten—and business on the street was bustling, despite him. With a heave, he lurched into an upright position, rubbing his face and getting his bearings. "What a shitty week," he thought.

Life had not always been so shitty. Then again, it had been shittier, and more dismal before, too. He remembered quite clearly November 1971, the hectic second week of the month that began with the assassination of his father, and ended with Fernando accepting the most dangerous job he had ever heard of. He remembered the old contact, Joseph, slapping him on the back, saying with a smile "Safer to be an Infantryman in 'Nam." The week was a mass of confusion; to learn of his Father's activities, to realize he, Fernando, better than any other, could step into the role. Saying yes to what seemed like a death sentence, suicide, but not suicide, because with everything he knew, did he really have a choice? For as understanding as Joseph seemed, he also gave the impression of being a man short on patience and without conscience. Such a man, of action, and absent morals, was not the kind to offer up choices.

Fernando remembered, those first few years, the ever present fear of his own shadow. The odd, seemingly meaningless missions. Requests for nonsensical information. The longer the process went on, the stranger and less threatening his occupation felt. Eventually, as the pay proved to be steady, and the accountability proved to be lax, and the dangers proved exaggerated, he started to feel like he alone was ahead at the table—that the middle man was the only one who could win. Certainly, there was the threat of catastrophe, and the possibility, on that day, of being finally called to task. But something about the process, the bizarreness of some of the happenings, made it all quite surreal. And so, quite comfortable.

Fernando worked his fingers across his forehead, trying to alleviate the hangover. Suddenly, after so long a hiatus, events that might call him to act. Is this how an agent was fired? They just broke contact, established another, and that was that? Could they afford to let a man, so integral to operations for decades, roam the streets unchecked, without fear of him acting from desperation? Was this new arrival his replacement, or his assassin, or both? Was it maybe a new contact, one who would find Fernando, when the time was right? Should he simply stay the course, stay vigilant, be prepared for the contact's directive? But why had he not been paid?

* * * *

Habana Viejo, a quadrant dedicated to the turistas, bustled in its usual mid-day way. With a calculated mix of Spanish-style squares, photo-op church facades, artists, food venders, book sellers and junket peddlers, the atmosphere seemed, to Sourdough, too balanced. Clean, cool stores offered the finest chocolates and cigars. Restaurants sprawled across the open squares, Son musicians floated their craft through the air, drawing in patrons looking to rest their feet a while, and maybe refresh with a chilled mojito. The merchandise available, for all its color and style, was decidedly of a limited theme—His image, His young lion, immortal, ferocious stare. You could take it back to your homeland on a bag, a shirt, a hat, a wristband. He drove the economy in a way, Gabrel reckoned, he would never approve of. But they purchased Him by the dozens, they displayed Him in the far corners of the world. And there were considerable positives in that.

Gabrel carried with him a notebook, the style for sale in any drug store, with the black and white speckled cover, the lined sheets within. He liked to walk, and observe, and then sit, and then write. Sometimes he wrote plainly of what he saw—sometimes, of the thoughts that came to him as a result of what he saw. And sometimes, he wrote of unrelated matters on his mind, unshakable images of last night's regrets, or correlations between them and long forgotten experiences. "It's all a daisy chain," Sourdough figured. "Unrelated as everything seems, it is all me, I am all it, there are connections here I cannot see."

He sat down on the steps of a church, watching the people walk by. Near him, further down on the slabs, a dark, black woman in a wildly bright, cultural dress, a flowing pattern that splashed about her, smoked an enormous cigar, asking for donations in exchange for photos. This church had probably been built by her ancestors, Gabrel thought. Slaves to the Spanish designers. He wondered when those slaves might have worn a dress like this. What occasion had they, what resources to craft it? There was something less than pure, something misleading in this image. But the smoke floating from the cigar made him want one, and a drink. The heat of the day had arrived, best spent either indoors or in the act of inebriation. Eventually, he wanted to tour both the rum and cigar factories, to study the process of fermenting the sugar and the art of rolling the tobacco leaves. Later, for the mind; now, the product, for the body. Sourdough scribbled down a few notes about the big black woman's smile, and the pattern of the cloth wrapped extravagantly round her head. Then he was on the move again.

*   *   *   *

He would not make it to any museums today, though he managed to find them all. The sandals he wore were from Mexico—not just made in Mexico, of course, as a pair of sandals worn by an Americano, they had a ninety-five percent chance of being manufactured south of the border. This pair, real leather, thick straps weaved in and out like a rug or pot holder, firm, his toes and heel exposed, but otherwise they might almost be shoes. That was a different excursion, years back, and the sandals showed their mileage. For the past several trips, he always kept an eye on the lookout for a replacement, something he could snatch the instant this pair gave way. But though they were torn and frayed, the buckle a bit loose, so they slipped and rubbed slightly around the ankle, they had earned their esteem. Sourdough had a sentimentality for clothing, or artifacts, that made it through journeys with him. He flew solo so often, so many interactions isolated, the sandals, the bracelets, the backpack—these inanimate objects were the only forces to know, entirely, where he'd been, what he'd done. So the sandals had earned the right to choose their last steps. They were destined for a trash bin somewhere, it was only a question of where. Perhaps that was why Gabrel felt such a bond with them.

He had wandered unintentionally out of the Viejo district, westward along the north shore, wrapping around the harbor to the Malecon, where the afternoon waves were encouraged by a strong breeze. In many places they splashed hard, up and over the wall, dousing the sidewalk, any pedestrians nearby, and sometimes all the way onto the road and the passing automobiles. Gabrel retreated across the stretch, to a bar on a corner with a nice view of the water. There were no other customers, the outdoor seating was windy, but the chairs were a sturdy quality, and he just wanted to jot some more notes. He ordered a mojito, and asked about cigars.

"Tengo Diplomaticos, senor. Esta bien?"

"Que bueno, si!"

The waitress was in her forties, pleasant, bringing forward a box of the long, dark cigars, lifting one tenderly to his ear, twirling it between her thumb and finger, inviting him to listen to the perfect crinkling sound of quality leaf against quality leaf. The atmosphere was fantastically chill, and after the mesera helped light the great roll, Sourdough sank into a mildly reflective, deeply relaxing zone. He was far too immersed in the hypnotic rhythm of the waves to pay notice to the local man gliding past, through the entrance, to a seat near the windows and away from the wind, inside. Raul ordered a beer, tenderly rubbing the muscles in his left foot as he waited for the drink. His mind was as capable as ever, but he'd been walking too much today.

He remembered that they used to have taxis on-hand. He would look into getting one tomorrow. Much had changed since then, resources redistributed, more emphasis and attention given to other departments. But when they heard that he'd already found the target—when they realized how capable he still was … Raul opened the can and took a satisfied drink. Then, one nonchalant glance at a time, he scanned his objective for details, putting together an initial report.

* * * *

The Diplomatico cigar was a long, sweet burn. With most, he inhaled conservatively, borderline faking it, letting the quick, hesitant puffs escape before the finely aged aroma had a chance to seduce his lungs. Yet every so often, due to the rum or daydream distractions, Sourdough would hold one for a respectable pause, with the roll facing into the wind, and a second dose charging his nostrils before the first had been released. Even seasoned cigarette smokers, the kind that support the industry and carry the musty smell to the grave, even they did not take an eight-inch long product of Cuba lightly. It was something to be appreciated, not rushed, and there was a certain way to squeeze maximum awe from the moment. But Gabrel knew nothing of that art, yet. He just felt a little bit high.

The slow burn dragged on, and the smoke scratched against his throat. It required near constant beverage support, and the mesera was up to the task. Eventually, the cigar still burning but Sourdough's lungs in retreat, he snuffed out the last portion, ashamed, rummaged sloppily through the pockets of his cargo pants for the cash to pay a bill of one Diplomatico and seven mojitos.

Raul was just about ready to give up, walk off, submit a report and gamble the boy would still be glued to that chair an hour down the road. A fortunate indecision, as he watched the Americano—this great threat—readjust his bearings and correctly—luckily—head toward the Centro.

Just as Raul rose to follow, the objective suddenly paused. Raul stayed frozen in place, half-standing, at best a blip in the far corner of Sourdough's peripheral vision. With a slight—wrong—change in direction, Gabrel stepped off, on his way. But instead of finishing the move, Raul returned to his chair. He looked down at his hands, pressing his palms flat against the table top, in an effort to stop the shakes.

For the first time, it occurred to him how arrogantly he was proceeding—and possibly to his doom. He was treating this new target like an amateur hack. This, a possible agent of the Enemy, and if so, a graduate of one of the most, if not the most, sophisticated international training programs in the world. A possible agent, selected from the cream of the crop, through a process involving thousands of dynamic people, all top graduates of esteemed academic institutions. This cream of the crop, having proven himself worthy of this assignment through demonstrations of exceptional physical and mental stamina under the harshest of training conditions, schooled in the most modern methods of operation, more dangerous with his bare hands than most people would be holding a loaded gun.

And Raul thought he could slide right by the objective, look him up in the data base, find where he was staying, guess his next move and discover him getting haphazardly drunk outside a dirty seaside bar. This was no game—and this target was certainly no Fernando. Ten minutes ago, Raul sat, bored, fantasizing of how impressed his superiors would be by his bang-up, no-sweat performance. Thirty seconds ago, he could have been killed, the highly-trained specialist carrying who knows what kinds of electro-weaponry in those cargo shorts, in that small back pack.

Raul felt suddenly out-matched. The problem with a profession such as this, he knew, was that you do not just throw in the towel, or admit weakness, or negotiate a compromise. He had not been asked to accept this challenge, he had been assigned an objective. The unstated understanding was as clear as the fact that they had not really asked him for very much, not for a very long time, and in essence, if this man was really as significant a concern to them as he seemed to be, they were finally asking him to earn his last decade's pay.

Reluctantly rising, he finally moved. Too risky to let the Americano disappear, and too risky to be anything less than on top of his game. This young wolf might have better training, but he could not have the street time. This wasn't his island. That was the one thing—the only thing—Fernando had going for him, in the beginning. Spy or no spy, this new one was still a turista.

Raul could spot a glimpse of his back, heading into the dense buildings of Habana Centro. From the opposite side of the street, he observed. Gabrel stopped now and then, every time as unsure as the last, but he never totally looked back, just around, in the windows, and at girls walking by. He was actually on the hunt for an internet café. Instead, he found new friends.

*   *   *   *

The ever-busy Calle Zapata divided Habana's Chinatown from the official Centro district, with a small cross street turning into a promenade alley and running its course through Centro, behind the Capitolo, in and out of darkness in the night—a trail well-traveled by many colorful figures. At the edge of Zapata, where it touched the start of the alley, a small cement park had been arranged. There were eight benches, some young, growing trees, and a stylish, if dull, Socialist sculpture. Night had fallen, and in the glow of streetlamps the creatures came out. Some were ambitious, like Lazaro, who stood with his pencil-thin arms crossed over his wiry chest cavity. Others were not so ambitious, like Sandra, who stood next to him, keeping steady balance on high heels, playing the eye-contact game.

As she had expected, Lazaro did not stop back in until morning. She woke at the sound of a footstep, and knew, at the sound, that he was not alone. Lazaro could sneak up on a mouse, shave the hairs off its back with a razor blade before it knew enough to rush away. The Frenchman's large hand still rested on her stomach. She reached across his back, carefully pulling some of the sheet over to her side, covering a little bit of her skin.

Lazaro stepped into the room, the light-skinned Latino girl, Danielle, by his side. She looked as though she had put her make-up on in a hurry. Sandra knew the difference. The Frenchman, she suspected, would not. Lazaro smiled at her, his old, steady eyes briefly passed over the whole scene, the parts the sheet covered, and the parts it did not.

"Wha' happen' in here?" his voice boomed good-naturedly, "Big par-ty, I think. Sum' body have big par-ty wif out me!"

The Frenchman woke and immediately began reaching for clothes, piece by piece, dressing quickly as he could. He was almost entirely suited, still sitting on the bed, Sandra still lying exactly as he'd left her, hours ago, when he finally noticed that Danielle had sat down on his other side, so he was between the two girls, whose ages combined nearly equaled his, on its own.

She had a nice smile, Sandra had even mentioned to her once, when they sat eating pizza; she liked how clean it was, the evenly thin lips, the way the style of her smile went well with her eyes. Danielle did not reply, just a nod. There were not many ways to respond.

Now she captured his full attention, and the absolute sleep must have revitalized the machinery. Seizing on the moment, Lazaro suggested desayuno.

"Not for Sandra, look at her, so tired, you make her so tired! We show mercy, let her sleep. Mercy for you, Sandra, rest and dreams."

Off they went to breakfast, Danielle wrapping an assuming arm inside the Frenchman's, guiding his hand to her hip. Of course this was only a tease; by the time they reached the door, Lazaro had very practically laid out a route and order of progress. The Frenchman went first, on his own, a wink exchanged with Danielle, no glance back toward the room where he slept. Sandra stood, beginning to dress, wondering if her abuelita was awake, if she still had only some crackers to eat.

As she slipped on her skirt, his hands joined from behind, guiding it over her knees, a light tug up over the thighs. With those skeletal fingers he zipped securely the back, turning her round with a grin, a playful, parental slap on the rear.

"I'll bring you back something. Wait here."

"Okay."

"Something spicy, and warm. Give you even more energy after some sleep."

"Okay."

"See you in an hour or two. Do me a favor, after your rest, take those sheets completely off the bed, lay them back on. Tuck the corners in tight. Nice and tight."

He walked back to Danielle, and they left.

* * * *

Sandra spotted Gabrel first, as he emerged unsurely from the Chinatown rows of restaurants. She had been dutifully playing the eye-contact game, which more or less meant attempting to make eye contact with every male that passed by unaccompanied. It was a given that they noticed her there, in those heels, and those firm-fitting jeans, her lean belly exposed, and a white long-sleeved top cut low in the front and giving off a light shine. So if they made eye contact, and held it for the slightest of moments, the event was no accident. For some it would be as courageous as they could ever get, as close as they would ever be to interacting with a woman like her. For so many others, the next step required only finding the right method of persuasion. Sandra's part was being available. Lazaro's was being himself.

Danielle had captured the attention of the Frenchman, and they by now were well acquainted, somewhere off in the dark. That freed Sandra from another night of the hand, but also meant playing this game. Many of the men walking by did not suite her. The Frenchman was at least from a cultured society; he had been places. Most of these options were beaten down bodies, faces that looked like they'd lived a life as a baseball glove, eyes wild enough to have scared her away, had Lazaro not been by her side. Still, she looked to them. And mostly they looked away. For so many different reasons, they looked away.

But he did not, and it happened with no warning. Perhaps she was staring, and he felt it, as sometimes we all can sense a stare. Regardless, when his swiveling head jerked toward her, and his eyes illuminated with recognition, Sandra could not look down fast enough—she did not look away fast enough. She wanted him not to recognize. And more, she wanted Lazaro to not notice the catch, even now as he boldly crossed the Calle Zapata, gesturing to the watch on his wrist, a schoolboy's naïve grin on his face. This was the kind of excitement she'd avoided for most of her life. This scene is explosive, she thought. "It can only end badly."

Like in the old days, when an opponent would lunge forward, throwing a hard right cross, or when they would pause in the middle of a round, needing to catch their breath, leaving a weak spot slightly exposed—no details escaped Lazaro. Before Sourdough could reach her, before he placed them all in a jeopardizing situation, the wiry old man intercepted his path. "Hel-lo, my friend, how you do-ing to-night?"

Gabrel gave a nod, but kept his eyes on Sandra. He at least stopped his approach, swinging left on the sidewalk. Lazaro and Sandra turned, too, keeping pace.

"My name is Lazaro. Where you from?"

"Los Angeles."

"Ah, America! Very good! Very good, man! This is Sandra. I am her uncle. How do you say this in English, cousin?"

"Niece. She's your niece?"

"Yes, niece! Great man, yes! Sandra likes to dance, very much. What is your name, man?"

Gabrel reached his arm across Lazaro, toward Sandra. He had stopped walking to do this, leaving them in an awkward, frozen position. Sandra shook his hand, remembering to keep her look on his eyes. Lazaro ushered them forward.

"You want to dance with her? With my niece? A very good club here, on this corner. You want maybe take her there, make her happy, watch her dance a little bit, man? What you think?"

Gabrel nodded, transferring his gaze to the negotiator for the first time. "What did you say your name was?"

"I am Lazaro. Come, man, let's go right here."

They stopped a little further down the block, where a minor, portable gate had been set up in a half-circle around the front entrance, two doors under an old neon sign proclaiming "Discotheque". Lazaro moved toward the door, maintaining a smile. "I will check if it is good night. Sandra is very good dancer, very good. I go and check. Excuse me, friend."

Lazaro went over to the doorman and began a conversation. In an instant, Sourdough moved forward, a bold step toward Sandra, leaning in close to ensure she could hear. "Donde esta su casa?"

"Como?"

He hesitated, and she watched the doubtful expressions as he double-checked the line in his head, then, sure it was what he intended, repeated the question.

"Donde esta su casa?"

Sandra kept her arms folded, gesturing with her eyes down the street, to the turn off toward the apartment. Sourdough kept his gaze steady on her, his voice strong with confidence. "Vamos."

"Si?"

"Si, vamos."

"Pero la discotheque-"

"No, no discotheque. Vamos ahora a su casa."

Lazaro returned to them just as Sourdough stepped back. Sandra explained what he'd said, but Lazaro did not believe it. They spoke in a rapid, colloquial style, and Gabrel did not bother to listen.

"He says he wants to go to the room, not to dance."

"How he said this to you?"

"He can speak some Spanish."

"Are you certain that was what he meant? How can you be certain that is what he meant?"

Lazaro turned to Gabrel with a smile, as if his exchange with Sandra had not happened. "The club is open, my friend. You want to watch Sandra dance, or maybe something else? She say you told her something, but she is not so sure. You want to go to my apartment, friend?"

Sourdough nodded. He tripped on the uneven steps as they walked, it was the first moment Sandra wondered if he was very drunk. But he recovered quickly, and they continued past the stores, and the pharmacy, Lazaro keeping him in conversation all the way.

"Where you stay, man?"

"Habana Centro."

"Yes, of course, but where, man? I know a good place, very good price, big, great place, great view, you want to stay there?"

"I have a place in Habana Centro."

"This place very good, man, you will love it, very good. I will show you if you want, I can call for you."

Lazaro guided the group, turning right, and into the sparse building, the entrance just slightly out of view of the thoroughfare. The emptiness of it, the darkness, the incredible amount of open, unused space within the sturdy outer structure pushed memories of last night to the surface of Gabrel's consciousness. He pushed them back into remission.

Lazaro's apartment was on the first floor of the building, straight ahead from the entrance. It consisted of three rooms in a row: a sort of foyer area, with a small two-person padded bench, then somewhat of a living area, where a few old chairs sat around a small, metal coffee table, and directly past that a room with a closet, a few shelves, and a bed, with a tiny bathroom area off to the side.

Sandra watched the Americano as they walked in. His eyes scanned the place—his eyes were very alive—but his expressions did not give any clues of surprise, or nervousness, or fear. She watched as he followed Lazaro into the third room, where they stopped beside the bed.

"What you want to do with my niece?"

"A lot of things. We can do them here?"

"Sure, sure, this is my place, no problem."

"But I want to be alone with her."

"Yes, yes, I go, I go in a minute, and the whole place is yours. But you know, Sandra, she is very beautiful, but she have nothing, man, very poor."

"Cuantos?"

"Ah, you speak Spanish! Very good man, very good! You can maybe speak with her, she would like that, man."

"Cuantos?"

"Its ok, no problem, I go. I don't know, man, what you want to do with her?"

"A lot of things."

"One hour, two hour? What, man?"

"Um, dos. Dos horas."

"Ok, is no problem, my place is yours, it is yours, you can sleep here if you want, man. You are my friend, man, Lazaro's friend, I take care of you. But she have nothing. What you want to give her?"

"Tell me."

"No, no. Whatever you think. What you think?"

Gabrel reached into his pocket, feeling for bills. He knew he had long since given away the power in this negotiation, and really did not care. Sandra looked fantastic, absolutely firm and well filled-out. The room was noticeably bare—nothing like his accommodation at the casa particular. The bed had only one sheet, the toilet, shielded by a slight wall, did not look like it worked, and the fact that Lazaro could return at any moment, catching him in numerous possibly compromising positions, would have been cause for concern if he wasn't so drunk.

"How about forty?"

"Forty?" Lazaro shrugged, acting like he did not care, as if any number would have been fine. "Sure, sure, is ok. I go, no problem, the place is for you and Sandra. I come back in two hours, and if you want to sleep here, is ok, you are my friend."

* * * *

Lying on her back, using the fingers of one hand to casually twist the curls of her hair, the other hand across her bare belly, Sandra noticed how much obnoxious noise Lazaro made in his entrance. At the sound of his booming voice coming through the front door, Gabrel pushed himself off of her, sliding instantly into his shorts. Sandra felt too good to move, wanting to just watch as he pulled on his shirt, over the pale, muscled chest and the left shoulder, with its strange tattoo. He was blinking a lot, she was not sure why, maybe trying to adjust to the light. It was not until her ears picked up the sound of ladies shoe heels clacking across the floor that Sandra also sat up, surprised by her own bashfulness.

"Hello, my friend. How you feeling?"

Lazaro entered, leaning against the wall, near the bed, with the grin of a man who just won the lottery. Standing beside him was Danielle. Sandra looked over at Sourdough, then down at her feet, and the floor, as his eyes went directly to the new girl, not Lazaro, and he puffed out his chest, straightening his broad back, before answering.

"Great."

Danielle gave him a smile, Lazaro nudged her with his elbow, and she moved across the room, her nice denim skirt cut high on her light-skinned thighs. Without acknowledging Sandra, she moved to Gabrel's other side, sitting, crossing her legs as she balanced her weight on the bed, he now sandwiched tightly between them.

"You tired, you want to sleep now?"

"No, no, I'm fine."

"You want to go for a drink, maybe? I know a very good place, very close, if you want a good drink. Would you like to take Danielle for a drink, maybe?"

Gabrel finally looked up at Lazaro.

"I'll take Sandra for one."

"Yes, yes, we all go, we all go. It is a very good place, my friend. Come, let's go. Sandra, Danielle." Lazaro motioned for the door as Sandra finished happily pulling on her clothes.

As a foursome they went back outside, into a very late night with few eyes on the empty streets. Back to the main calle, directly across it, on a corner property, was a six-story hotel, its walls painted pink. Lazaro gestured to a pair of double doors around the side. "There is the entrance. Come, my friend. Did I tell you I was a boxer, eh? You know Olympics, my friend?"

Gabrel looked down at his watch, Sandra noticed he had finally stopped blinking. "It's late. You think this place will even be open?"

"This bar, always open, always. Is part of this hotel, and is always open, no problem."

"What is the name of this place?"

Lazaro opened, the door, sweeping them all into the dimly lit room. "This is the Hotel Lincoln. Is very good, good mojitos. You like mojito, yes?"

There was a large black man in a black suit, his thick arms barely fitting through the sleeves. He greeted Lazaro with a slight tilt of the head. In the next room, set off as a side room from the reception area, a man in a beige, collared shirt stood behind the bar, watching a video on the television. A white, foreign-looking man sat on a stool next to a woman with dyed-blonde hair in a shiny pink dress. Both the bartender and the girl gave Lazaro a nod, as he led his party to a table in the corner, a wave of his hand telling the mesero to report. For the first time, Sandra noticed, the Americano looked uneasy. He spoke quietly to Lazaro.

"Don't tell them where I am from."

Lazaro patted the Americano's forearm assuredly. "Of course, of course, is no problem. That man over there, he is from Australia. He is having a good time, just like you!"

First, Lazaro suggested a round of mojitos, and Sourdough agreed without pause. He was eager to explain his plans, his interest in the Revolution, and wanting to see a baseball game. Sandra listened intently as, with every statement, he would first turn to her, trying to explain in Spanish. She would listen as hard as a person could, wanting so badly to get it, but inevitably just giggling, shaking her head, rubbing his leg with her hand under the table as he insisted on explaining in English, and waiting for Lazaro's translation to the girls. It was their reaction to his humor that he wanted to see, and Lazaro, his eyes shining, gladly played middle man. The Americano's face was a bright anticipating smile, his sandy brown hair still a ruffled mess, his cheeks scruffy with a prickly three-day beard that had felt like sandpaper scratching her body.

Lazaro asked Gabrel to buy some cigarettes, and the Americano agreed. The bartender brought the pack over, and Lazaro asked if they should order another round of drinks. Sourdough glanced back toward the music video on the small t.v., but really he was looking over at the Australian. He said sure, of course, but after that, maybe they should go. Sandra would have preferred to drink water, if mojitos meant ending the night. But she was not the musician, as Lazaro had once said, "playing the lead violin."

Indeed, the Americano had many plans. He said he would be in Cuba for two weeks, not just Habana but all across the island. He wanted to see tobacco plantations, and cigar rolling factories. He wanted to see sugar plantations, and do a walking tour of a rum museum, to understand the process. He wanted to go to Santiago, the Eastern coast, and into the mountains there, to see for himself where the Revolution was born. When he spoke of these things, his eyes were round and wild, his hands and arms flailing with gestures through the air. It was a little bit funny, to Sandra, for an American, of all people, to be so curious about a little island where he had no family. Lazaro assured him all was possible, and spoke of the activities as though they would complete the checklist in tandem. "We will go to a baseball game." "We will see the cigar factory, yes."

Gabrel pulled out his tour book, showing them his map of the city, the locations of the museums, monuments, and known places he hoped to investigate. Lazaro once again asked where he was staying, and Sourdough pointed to a small star he had drawn in black pen, leading everyone to a good laugh, even the girls, as Lazaro showed then where they were sitting, only two blocks away, just around a few corners.

The Americano seemed relieved he would not have a very far walk, rising in an instant of energy, signaling the bartender, paying the bill for the party. As they left the hotel, Lazaro again offered his place for the night. As they walked past the place, Lazaro insisted they escort him all the way to his casa particular. As they arrived at the door, Sourdough found himself agreeing to meet Lazaro again in the morning, around ten, to at least check out the "better, cheaper" apartment "penthouse" the wiry little man insisted he would love.

Before they left, he pulled her close for a last, intense kiss, the kind meant to squeeze an hour's worth of full-body passion into a ten second spurt, like trying to gush a whole river through a small crack in a dam. Then he found his key, and disappeared into the officially licensed place.

On the short walk back to Lazaro's, Sandra could not contain her thoughts, something she normally did so well. Recalling for them the funny moments in the bar, laughing to herself, remembering how he had tripped on the way there. Danielle just walked, and Lazaro just listened. He had pulled out a cigarette, and lingered outside, finishing his smoke, as the two girls went in to the bed. Crouched down on the concrete steps, listening to a few Soviet motors still working the street, he realized the sun would be up in an hour.

Day 4

Comandante Barbuda sucked another glob of orange juice through the plastic straw, shifting it around in his mouth with his tongue. As he set the glass down, the nurse dutifully refilled it, and then he sipped up some more. He was feeling especially energetic, revived by the morning's report.

They had tracked down quite a bit of background information on the new operative. With today's technology, a library of detail was available at the touch of a few buttons, on any citizen of any country, the moment their passport number was typed into the international tracking system. In this instance, however, there were variables.

Cuba did not adhere to the same system used in most parts of the developed world. Not because they lacked the equipment, but out of respect for the individual traveler. So the first variable, for an American arriving at Jose Marti International Airport, was that as a matter of national security and out of distrust of the opposition government, the secret of the traveler's arrival stayed between them and the sovereign nation of Cuba. This meant not entering their passport code into the system, which opened a need to unearth their background through other means.

And those "other means" meant coordinating with the moles, multiple moles, overlapping areas of interest, cross-checking each other, three for every one job, just to make sure. They were worth every penny on the bankroll each time a traitor was revealed. Some were not traitors; simply lazy, unpatriotic men. But the reliable ones would respond with vigorous determination, reporting nothing until they had verified the source, fully aware that every word they sent carried an understood vow. They were swearing accuracy and truth, on their lives.

So it understandably took a little time to fact check Senor Gabrel Sourdough, knowing the enemy's knack for creating false identities, false lives, all the way back to false grandparents living in false small towns. Comandante Barbuda flipped over a page in the portfolio, sliding his fingers along the edges of the passport photo. A pair of steady, unimpressed eyes on a young, clean-shaven face looked up at him, almost daring Barbuda to make the next move. They were making a pretty cocky statement, sending this one. They were putting a rookie pitcher on the mound.

To the inexperienced eye, the moles had turned up nothing. A college degree in a meaningless field, idle time squandered traveling, no record—or gaps in the timeline that could support it—for intelligence agency academies and seasoning field work. Just a curious young man dropping in on a forbidden vacation spot. Maybe an oddly-focused adrenaline junkie with some spare time on his hands. There was no reason to believe he could even speak Spanish, to keep himself afloat if he wandered out of Habana Viejo.

Except, last night, he did. The submitted report detailed time spent along the Malecon, not far, actually, from the U.S. Special Interest building, though he mostly lingered at a café. It also described a late night excursion into the Centro district, though apparently all he did was walk around a little bit, eat some Chinese food, then return to his casa particular for sleep. Not the most active of evenings, which also alarmed Comandante. The agent might be stalling, biding his time; waiting for a designated event. And it was that very possibility that had Barbuda so energized this morning. An event he had not even disclosed to his staff; a secret between him and an old drunken ghost.

Known, somehow, by his nemesis?

* * * *

Fernando emerged from a guided pack of tourists, their leader walking backwards, explaining the origins of the nearby church in German. He had worked his way slowly, the process covering hours, until Raul had sat down to a late breakfast, finally, here. Thinking on his feet—sober now, for almost a whole day, Fernando muscled into the center of the group, keeping his head low, peering between the shoulders and necks of the photo-crazed visitors. Now he stood only three steps—a good lunging distance—directly behind Raul, who looked too busy perusing the menu to take note.

As Fernando rehearsed his clever opening line, the menu was thrown down on the table. Raul rose, cocking his head back as he tossed a last gulp of coffee down his throat, storming away with the stalking form of a furious gorilla on a hunt. His fists were clenched, his arms tensely flexed; the movements of a man who truly wanted to break into a sprint, but knew it would raise too much fuss. Fernando, slouching, demoralized and a bit in awe of his old chess companion, watched Raul march out of site. He was heading toward the Capitolo, and certainly for a reason connected to this new agent, and therefore connected to Fernando's own fate.

He ran the circumstances, the knowns and the unknowns, through his tired head all night. The decision to track down Raul, to confront him, came from a lack of alternatives. But he did not know what to say, or how to posture himself in a way to get the information he needed. There was a chance—especially now, seeing how active and absorbed Raul was—that the Cuban Government had learned quite a bit; that they were not grasping grains of sand the way he was. Yes, Raul appeared totally in his prime, only further depressing Fernando.

He had to be straight with himself: there was a small sense of relief that the confrontation did not happen. Fernando did not feel ready for it. He needed to go cold turkey on the booze, to start thinking straight. There was a chance his mind was not as sharp as the old days, but there was no advantage to accepting this angle. Fernando sat down, ordered a coffee, and asked also for paper and pen. He did not attend the schools of the privileged; he earned his position by deed. "If you exercise the body, it grows stronger," he thought. "If you exercise the mind, it will, too."

To be totally straight, he also had to acknowledge the other, small reason for his relief. Whether he was being paid or not, whether the new operative was there to replace, or assassinate, or use and discard him—he remembered the directive, now decades ago, reminding him that he was accepting a position and duties that he would be obligated to perform honorably "until further notice". No message of termination, through any avenue, had passed his way. Because of this, despite how much better he thought he knew and understood Raul compared with his employer, his stomach felt a little sick over the idea of appealing to the competitor for assistance saving his own neck, when such a move might compromise a much more important action. This was a bothersome thought, and another reason for Fernando's growing appreciation that the moment had been postponed.

* * * *

Gabrel rose after only three hours with veins still fueled by adrenaline. The shower, high-powered and a perfect warmth, soothed his shoulders and back like a professional Thai masseuse. Before heading out, he packed his things, telling the house owner he would probably be back in a few hours, and probably just to pay and move on.

Amid the morning activities, dodging bicycles and maneuvering around fruit vendors whose fragile tables blocked the narrow sidewalks, he retraced the past evening's steps, passing Lazaro's apartment building—no signs of movement around there—out onto Calle Zapata, the wide street a bustle of movement, scratchy music floating out of small radios, and the buzz of conversation in a language barely decipherable. Gabrel turned, hiking to the spot across from Chinatown where he'd met them, realizing a decent, low-cost restaurant was there, serving desayuno. They even had café latte, which he gladly ordered, pulling out his black and white spotted notebook and making a record out of his thoughts. He had a couple hours before meeting them. Instead of walking around, more exploration, Sourdough elected to leave that for later. Putting a thoughtful note in the ledger at least once a day felt good. Besides that, he was hoping for a mid-afternoon session with Sandra, and was worried his fatigue might soon come to bear.

The latte tasted fantastic. It probably could have been a bucket of warm, dirty sea water and he still would have pronounced it his new favorite beverage. It was one of those mornings, reflective not just of his satisfaction with the previous night, but of the long drought since the last time he had felt so deeply involved in a worthy adventure. He knew there would be times on this island when the locals would build up a barrier, when he wouldn't be able to convince them to let down their guard, and when everything from asking directions to attempting small talk in a bar would feel more like a business transaction with a negotiated fare. The past night had its fares, but made up for them with its rawness. Hustlers weren't always humane; the effort rarely advanced their interests.

Gabrel's pen dashed across the pages, little notes scribbled between lines he would come back to, remembering more detail and wanting it preserved. At most of the other tables, local men conversed, in no hurry, off in no direction. Then he realized he was, most certainly, the only white person in the joint. And the latte tasted fantastic.

* * * *

Sourdough moved down the sidewalk, sliding by pedestrians like a halfback in a video game, keeping his eyes focused straight ahead, trying not to look like he was running away from something while getting as far away from the scene as he could. A few turns, a few blocks, and he should be back at the casa particular. Hopefully the owner was still there. Hopefully he could have his old room another night.

He had meandered back past Lazaro's place a few minutes early, but thought "What the hell", walked up to the door and knocked. Sandra opened it, in a nice summer dress, the top red and spaghetti strapped, the bottom half made of dark blue denim. She looked as good as she had the night prior, Sourdough hoping that she was alone. But Lazaro came forward from the back bed, with the dry, thirsty look of a man in the middle of sleep.

While Gabrel sat in an old patio chair, and Sandra stood beside him, her belly near to his head, Lazaro made a phone call on his old, blue mobile, pulling on a new shirt, smoking another cigarette. He finished the call, quickly brushed his teeth—enough time out of the room for Sourdough to give Sandra a quick kiss, wondering at his own shyness in front of a man who had seen them together in bed the past night, both still sweating and smelling of sex. The daylight and sobriety seemed to reset the code of conduct, and when Lazaro returned to the room, Gabrel nudged Sandra away.

The last evening they had moved with such freedom; having no prior experience with protocol, Sourdough felt no worries as the three of them stepped into the sunlight. But in rapid blips of confused action, the situation crashed. He remembered that his arm was around Sandra's waist, and he now almost remembered her trying to push it away. He remembered Lazaro walking a few steps in front, and he now almost remembered him stepping directly toward someone specific, someone he recognized, and beginning to speak. Sourdough remembered looking up, and seeing four uniformed policia, standing in a line, a human barrier preventing the natural flow of traffic from the side street onto Calle Zapata. He now almost remembered that the four pairs of eyes, in the four matching brown uniforms, were all looking at them—not at him, but at Lazaro and Sandra. They had been waiting, and now collapsed on their prey, all in a surreal moment as Gabrel felt himself separate from Sandra, drift to the right, away. He could feel his facial expression turn to something nonchalant, unconcerned, and detached. Having never been in a similar situation before—not even sure what kind of a situation this was—he knew instinctively not to look back, not to listen to any sounds, any possible directions being shouted at him. It was obvious he was foreign—there was no more reason to assume he understood Spanish than there was to assume these foot-soldier policia could muster a phrase in English. Deaf to the world, he walked with a determined pace to the right, down the sidewalk, buzzed and brainstorming what he would do if he could not return to the room.

Had he been watching, Gabrel would have seen Lazaro trying to argue his case. He would have seen Sandra, without the slightest hint of surprise, anger, or any other emotion, obligingly move into the back seat of the police vehicle. He would have seen Lazaro do the same, still trying to explain, hands wildly gesturing, while he scanned the onlooking crowd, hoping to spot the Americano, hoping he had not lost him just yet. As the car drove away, Lazaro kept going, thinking of different angles, trying to touch a nerve that might be helpful the next time around. He spotted Sourdough's back, the young man's body bouncing as he moved quickly down another street. Lazaro smiled. The Americano was not a lost cause. But he needed to intercept him again, this afternoon, before someone else did.

*   *   *   *

Raul, his arms crossed over his chest, stood close to the window, watching the young jinitera in the other room. He did not even try to sleep the night before; there was no way that was going to happen. Letting crazy, stupid instinct guide him into submitting the first intentionally misleading report of his entire career, he knew that today would likely be his final one on the job. Maybe his last day alive. And the determining factor, aside from his own foolishness, might be this young girl, sitting there, staring at the blank wall.

Why did he not report the event up to Higher? Why did he downplay the evening with imagined detail, instead of the truth? He had followed, he had seen everything. The only directive was to accurately report where the operative went, what the operative did. Sometime during the hours spent watching, monitoring movement, knowing full well what goes on in rundown apartment buildings on side streets, what kind of people linger in the early hours at the Hotel Lincoln bar, Raul had become skeptical. Something here wasn't quite right. The scenario did not add up. And as the observer on the ground, he wanted more transparency before typing words into a report, to be judged and acted aggressively on by shadowy figures in the shadowy buildings where the report would finally be read. He was taking an awfully big risk on this project, on these people.

They released the old man right away. Raul did not know him, but the station manager did. Said his name was Lazaro, something about being an old boxer, a long time ago, now a hustler who knew a lot of girls, a lot of people in general. From the moment he was led into the station, through the processing line, he was talking, negotiating, labeling the event a misunderstanding, talking of discrimination and unfair treatment in a way very few would dare. The thin little man with the salty grey hair and weather beaten face irritated the hell out of Raul. He did not want to see him, or interrogate him. He did not want to know why the operative would even talk to such a piece of scum. True to what Raul suspected, Lazaro left quickly, soon as he was released. No questions on the fate of the girl. No thought of sticking around and waiting for her, or lobbying for her release.

The station manager looked over the files, stating she, too, had been there before. They already held her identification card, and this arrest would mean they would keep it longer still. Raul studied her face, searching for a hint of a sign of frustration or impatience or nerves. She could not even know that Lazaro was gone—as if they had an understanding in such situations, a strategy of total separation.

"How old is she?"

"The record says nineteen, sir."

Raul looked over at the manager, a chubby man with an unpolished star pinned onto a shirt pocket. No one had called him 'Sir' in about twenty years. "She has always been associated with that man?"

"To my knowledge, yes, sir." The manager shifted his weight, closing the file and extending it to Raul. "Would you like a word with her?"

"I haven't decided yet."

"I mean, sir, a private word? Perhaps to help you decide what you want to ask her about?"

Raul turned his eyes back to the man. Somehow he looked fatter, even more pathetic now. What he most resembled was a child in line at a candy store, or a cow stuck behind others at the trough at feeding time. It occurred to Raul that the longer he kept the young woman in custody, the more vultures in the office took notice, circling in their own wicked ways. When he was through, he would have to release her himself, or the girl would end up doing what she probably had to endure the last time; earning her way to the exit. He looked at her again, finally feeling a good hunch about the workings of her mind.

* * * *

Lazaro had guessed right. The Americano had mentioned this spot last night, as they escorted him back to his casa particular. The corner bar was operated by his friend, Miguel, who confirmed the visit, on Lazaro's description. From the police station he had come straight here, spoken to his old associate, then sat on a stool and joined into the talk of the day, which was, to no surprise, the Industrial's new manager.

There were other errands to run, but he let the hours pass by. All his life, he had been a man of great energy. He used to boast that you could ask any woman between the ages of fifteen and fifty-five in Habana, they would attest to his stamina with a blush and a smile. In the ring, his opponents always tired first—always. The international amateur matches were usually only three rounds, anyway. Lazaro often said he would train for nine straight hours, throwing punches, slipping jabs, drilling footwork nine straight hours, to be sure he could out-perform his opponent for nine ferocious minutes. Having that much natural energy meant needing ways to burn it off, wanting to be on the move, in motion, working deals, making money. He was not the type to waste an afternoon lying in bed, staring up at the ceiling, like so many of his girls always did. He was not the type to spend that time glued to a stool in a bar, either, like so many Cubanos he knew.

The bad luck in his life always seemed God's way of keeping his energy in check. The disqualification at the '72 games in Mexico City. The way so many pig officials targeted him, wanted to make an example of him, do everything they could to stop him from being the very thing they wished they were—free, to be drunk when he wished, to be stoned when he wished, to be pleasured by a young, warm-blooded girl when he wished. What they wanted was his energy, and his guts. But they had all been born weak, so they wanted to bring him down, too.

Finally, Sourdough came walking, from the direction of the Capitolo, his small pack slung over one shoulder, the same notebook from the morning carried in his left hand. He did not look as concerned as before, probably let the scene filter out of his mind, now back for a rest after checking out more of those landmarks annotated on the map in his book. Lazaro approached like an arrow, but also like a priest; his arms extended, palms up, as apologetic and merciful a pose as he could muster.

Less than a minute of talking was necessary to convince the Americano that it all had been a big misunderstanding, that he should not have fled as he did, that there was really not much to explain. Gabrel was not very happy to see him, but did not have a good reason to verbally abuse his only connection to Sandra, whose own condition he was very concerned about.

"Oh, she's ok, ok, she was worried for you! She asked, 'Where he go? Is he angry with me?'"

"Where is she?"

"Sandra is fine, she is fine. You want I show you the apartment now? Is very nice, Sandra see it, her eyes go big, she like it so much. And she can stay with you there, is no problem. There, no problems, man."

The penthouse turned out better than the boasts. It was the rooftop of the tallest building around, fourteen floors up in an elevator the size of a shoebox, secured further by a locked gate at the level. This meant that any unwelcome visitor might find someone to let them enter the building, might have the fortune to find the lift operating, but when they reached the floor, would need the good graces of the tenant to let them pass. Gabrel had not yet begun to appreciate the value in this feature.

Even though there was no official sticker, no official standards adhered to, the quality of the place vastly surpassed the single room and shared bath and shower Sourdough had enjoyed for the last few nights. There was a living room, with a television, a spacious couch, more cushioned chairs set around it. There was a dining table, very proper looking, with a display case of fine plates and porcelain dolls. The room where he would sleep had two beds, air conditioning, good water power and a toilet that flushed. There was a kitchen, where breakfast would be prepared.

Many certified casa particulars could claim similar if not better accessory accommodations. But when Gabrel walked out onto the sprawling patio, overlooking the Centro district, all the way to the sea, Lazaro began to appear less like a crafty hustler, and more like an incredibly valuable resource.

Waiting to meet them, and giving the tour, was Young Samuel. Bare-chested, well-tanned, in surfer shorts, a bracelet slipped around the left ankle and Rastafarian braided hair, he greeted Sourdough with a warm smile. He looked to be mid-twenties, and far more chilled out than any Cuban male encountered yet on the trip. He looked like a beach bum from SoCal, not a nursing student interning at the hospital. But that, he explained, was what he was, and the casual way he led them around made the scenario seem even more perfect. This was obviously a helluva good guy.

Young Samuel's English was better than basic, though he struggled with pronunciation. It took a few repetitions to communicate that he was Young Samuel, and this was not really his place to rent. It belonged to his Grandfather, "Old Samuel", who did not speak English, and would be around later. They lived in a few small rooms off to the side of the rooftop. They would prepare the breakfasts, maybe watch a little television in the evening, but "the place is yours, man, whatever you want to do."

Before Gabrel had even agreed, Young Samuel gave him the keys. He had to go meet some friends for some futbol, just a pick-up game, he would be back after dark. He shook Lazaro's hand with a nod of respect, left, and Lazaro fell back into a spot on the couch, looking up at Sourdough with a "told you so" wink. The Americano, very pleased, walked back outside to admire the view.

* * * *

Fernando was not raised with religion, like many of his friends. He knew that his mother had been, but the circumstances in her life, the dramatic shifts, emotional turbulence, stripped her of a desire to rely on deities, or assign them with credit or blame. His friends grew up in houses decorated with alters for icons, beads and paintings and prayer cards. With age, his curiosity went away. He was no Communist, but he had to admit, some of their principles were at the very least reasonable.

This led to his opinion on ghosts. It was hard to believe in them, to believe in spirits, especially the kind you could interact with, and not have any view to one side or the other regarding an afterlife, or a higher power. For most of Fernando's life, there was no conflict in this. But the first night the spirit addressed him, his choices changed from whether or not to believe in God, to whether or not to believe himself sane.

The visits were not regular. Rare enough, in fact, to be brushed off as side effects to drinking binges. The flaw in the theory was that Fernando tended to drink most heavily when he was under a lot of pressure, or in a tight spot. So maybe, for these desperate times, he subconsciously did not fight the natural human habit to want guidance from Above, evidence of a helping hand in the cosmos to guarantee that not only was he important, but it was all happening for a reason toward the collective good. Clever, and maybe unsurprising, for him to replace a crucified prophet with an alcoholic American. A very clever lie of the mind.

The more he thought about it, the more he should have been expecting another drop-in. If he was still sharp, he would have expected it. If he was still on his game. Hopefully the spirit came to explain, and not just to drink all his rum.

"You look a tad rough, Fernando. You should think about getting a haircut."
"I need more than a haircut."
"A strong drink, before you go?"
"I'm off the stuff for now. I need to get sharp."
"Tell a fella why?"
"The same reason I'm imagining you here."
"What reason'd that be?"
"When I'm sharp, I'll let you know."
"What are you gonna do about it?"
"Once I know what it is, I'll know what to do."
"Sure the juice won't get you there faster?"
"Recognizing you are full of shit is the first sign I'm coming around."
"I'll toast you on that one!"

Fernando sighed. Time was of the essence, he could sense it. For the longest while he had felt very comfortable floating along, submitting the status quo reports, never wondering too seriously if they were read, never wondering too deeply his employer's opinion of his performance. There had been one other instance, in '91, when the air on the streets buzzed electric, anticipation of some sort of internal collapse, or coupe d'etat, felt imminent for all the wrong reasons. What Fernando remembered most was how rapid back-channel communication flowed during those few weeks. They wanted to know everything from the number of military trucks passing a certain point, per hour, to the number and type of stores and businesses still open after dark. All along, often running on adrenaline and a little bit of fear, Fernando had let one possibility take root in the far back of his mind: they had absolutely no idea what was happening. They had absolutely no idea how the political collapse in Eastern Europe would resonate and affect a small island whose leaders already seemed clinging to the edge of a high cliff. They had theories, but by that point, after all that time, their theories were really just guesses, built on the foundations of other theories, and so on, so forth, back to only a few semi-concrete morsels of information, confirmed by sources long since killed or retired. In a lot of ways, Fernando felt like a guide dog, with a blind master who did not really know where he wanted to be led, or what he wanted to encounter. Maybe that was why they so often stayed inside; where ignorance could be clung to like a warm security blanket.

The ghost was still in the room—which could have meant any number of things concerning Fernando's state of being. "Not that I particularly care, but since you don't seem to be leaving, what would you do?"

"If you're in a cage with a lion, you need to be a wilder lion."

"What if you're in a cage with a lamb?"

"Then be the wildest lion you can. That lamb's known its fate since the day it was born."

"I don't think the world's so black and white anymore."

"Your perspective has changed, not the object you're looking at. Now's the time to go on the offensive, before they recognize you as a threat."

"And if they already do?"

"You know the answer to that, bud."

Fernando did know the answer. If he was already a part of the equation, he needed to dramatically change his performance; to contradict their expectations, foul up their entire plan. "Do you think I'm wrong to look out for myself?"

"What a stupid thing to ask."

* * * *

Gabrel woke from his nap feeling spectacular. The air-conditioning unit produced a steady buzz to go with the cool air, functioning as just the right level of white noise to block out everything else. He pushed himself up on his side, resting on a forearm and looking at himself in the mirror on the bathroom door. No question he came here to submerge in the reality of the place. No question he was at least shoulder-deep already. Time management was going to be a tough thing from here on; hard to soak in the sites and information at the daytime-only tourist spots and also absorb the blade-running thrill of the spicey, shady nights. Rather than decide, he would let events and opportunities pull him along. It was the only respectable way to go.

Leaving his room, riding high on this cloud of philosophy, Sourdough could feel the wave break out beneath him, give way, as he found Lazaro playing chess against Sandra. A pleasant surprise, still in the morning's dress, looking no worse for wear. But Lazaro, reclined in a chair, moving a rook, appeared even more relaxed, as though he was as natural a piece of the picture as the couch and the porcelain dolls.

The old boxer began talking of plans Gabrel did not recall making. Of dinner, a night at the discotheque, describing how he would teach Sourdough to dance, how good that he'd had time to rest, because once Sandra made it to a dance floor, she would stay on it as long as she could, and the inexperienced American would need all the energy he might muster to keep up. Gabrel realized that from the beginning, which was really not even twenty-four hours ago, he had wanted to like Lazaro. He was hot for Sandra, and friendly relations with this old man, her "uncle", who seemed to know a great deal about the things Gabrel wanted to know a great deal about, too, sounded like good policy all the way. Sandra was a very nice girl. The penthouse was a galactic improvement, beyond any backpacker expectations. Access to a man who had been around for "it all", and possessed both the English and the desire to describe and explain what really occurred, was too tempting to pass on. You don't read a book if you have the chance to talk to the author.

But a stipulation in the arrangement was becoming uncomfortably clear. Lazaro was far more interested in developing his own relationship with the young foreigner than in fostering Sandra's. And he was not offering the American information to guide his adventure, he was offering himself as an attached tour guide. The kind you take with you to dinner, and to discos, and apparently to your apartment. And now, having swallowed the bait with a voracious, naïve gulp, Gabrel realized this man had him good.

He'd been planning on spending three days in the city. When they got to the penthouse, and he saw the view, and imagined the possibilities, he began flirting with making it at least a week. No sense in rushing off to the countryside, back into the struggles of starting fresh, when this fortuitous scenario fell right in his lap.

Now, with Sandra moving to the television, flipping through channels, and Lazaro waiting for an answer on what time they should go, what style of food Gabrel wanted to eat, his previous experiences, thus far dormant, kicked in, and an egg of an escape plan began to incubate.

* * * *

Comandante Barbuda tried not to cringe or show any of the discomfort he felt as the two aids shifted his body weight back and forth, lifting an arm at a time, shoving it into a sleeve, and gradually fitting him into the lounge jacket, ready for the photo op. The mid-afternoon was too hot for this, there were reasons for him wearing the light, soft pajamas. He opened his mouth to reprimand them, to criticize the entire effort, but stopped, remembering this was all his idea. Lately he was taking extra care not to ridicule underlings for the mistakes of their masters.

Another reason for the heat and discomfort was the number of unwanted people in his room. Aside from the aides, there was the photographer, with the kind of big box camera you only saw at weddings, and hardly even there anymore. He, of course, had an assistant, switching lenses, fiddling with light aperture, quietly making suggestions regarding placement, this figure here, that one over there, maybe we should add a table and some drinks. At Barbuda's request, his personal body guard, normally on call somewhere in the hallway, was seated in the corner; his large, brooding presence a visual reminder to the rest of them that this all could be canceled, and they all could be sent out, at the lift of a finger.

Then there was the reason for the occasion, and his entourage. He stood near the window, looking out, wearing a fine Italian suit, soft leather shoes, and a gigantic gold watch wrapped like a fat boa constrictor around his left wrist. His tediously styled black hair was slicked back to symmetrical perfection, and a big, toothy grin dominated the round, light brown face as he spoke casually with an advisor. Finally the aides stepped back, nodding to each other, satisfied with the results of the molestation. They signaled the photographer, who notified his assistant, who rushed over to the advisor, who whispered into the suited man's ear. Everyone took their positions, the video and still-photo cameras started rolling and clicking, and the gentleman walked like an Emperor across the room, toward Comandante, like an old battle buddy back from the grave, or a cousin from childhood fresh out of prison.

When the man spoke, his eyes reverently focused on Barbuda, yet his words sounded like a bad song, sung far away, for an audience far away. When it was Comandante's turn, to give the advice of a front-line soldier, or of a mountain climber, on his way down from the summit, passing on pointers to a newbie just setting out from the basecamp, the man in the fine Italian suit nodded, but his eyes were as far away as the song. He waited for Barbuda to finish a thought, turned to his advisor, and suggested a new angle for a new round of photos. The advisor directed the adjustments, and the photographer complied with high energy; as though the order came down from his own leader, and not just an ambitious foreign dignitary.

Comandante could have raised his finger, he could have set his personal guard into a room-clearing, sweeping action. Instead he let his mind drift, to a place where it would tell him no lies.

"If my ally believes me irrelevant, what must my enemy think?"

He would stay in the chair, keep his mouth shut, finish the session, and wish the man well. Perhaps if it were only the two of them in the room, perhaps if he thought he had the man's attention, or that the man was more interested in advice than the resolution of the film, it would be worth grabbing his arm, squeezing it to show what strength, what power still lived in him. Giving him the iron stare that had ended so many arguments, showing him the fire that still burned in the sockets. Shattering the man's unwarranted ego with a boom of the voice that had rocked rallies and public gatherings for half a century, just to remind the man that the difference between an Italian suit and a set of old pajamas was that anybody can show up in the former, but you know your salt when you can command a room, or a nation, in the latter. Perhaps if they were alone, he would give the advice the man did not even realize he needed. Instead, Barbuda thought about his enemy. The enemy was the one to remind, in a way to guarantee that he never forgot again.

*　　*　　*　　*

Raul's own dishonesty in reporting made him decide not to bring anyone else onto the project. He did not want to risk trusting any eyes but his own to watching the apartment building, monitoring the comings and goings, following the operative and dealing with him accordingly. As it stood, he was trying to figure out ways to phrase the newest update to make the morning's arrests seem unrelated, and the target's decision to switch housing a mere economics-based decision. They would know the lodging was unauthorized—he would need to persuade them not to interfere, to let the situation play out. They would wonder how he had found an out-of-the-books place, what role the proprietor—this Samuel—might play in the overall scenario. He had worked himself into a corner with the misinformation, and now could not risk bringing another pair of hands into the mix, and hope they would understand and subscribe to his rationale.

The girl, this Sandra, seemed harmless enough when he finally spoke to her at the station. He decided not to ask any specific questions about the American, and felt confident she left thinking it just another petty hassle. Much as it sickened him to do it—feeling even more disgusted with himself now, thinking back—Raul determined it prudent to grope her a little on her way out the door, to further encourage in her mind the idea he was just another asshole, passing the time on a slow day by exercising his power over the weak. She had not flinched, or turned her gaze from the doorknob. He tried his most devilish grin, but the shame, young enough to be his daughter. He turned away, and she left. At the time, he considered her a side-note, and had been glad he kept her out of official documents.

He followed her, to the tall apartment building, and at first thought she was just going home. But she reappeared on the rooftop, with Lazaro, then eventually Lazaro slipped out, exiting the building and heading his own way around sunset. By then, the American could be seen, relaxing in a chair, with a notebook, scanning the skyline, talking with Sandra, and then the two of them sitting down with a much older, strong-looking bald man. Raul quickly learned this was Samuel, a fellow with a long, questionable history. Suddenly, and sadly, Sandra did not seem so insignificant—neither did Lazaro.

Records revealed Samuel to be an old Batista-army veteran. Most men his age, still alive, were young, insignificant at the time of the Revolution, and were not punished for their service, since they played no great role. But this Samuel had served in the Presidential Guard, a position acquired through rapid promotion at an inexperienced age. The unit disbanded, every man for himself, when El Presidente fled into exile. The rest were all tried for harsh crimes. Samuel had only served in the duty position for a few weeks, and was pardoned.

Raul re-read the second page of the file, rotating his attention between the information and the living room light of the penthouse apartment. Samuel had married, moved on, into civilian work. Mostly simple labor, some factory time, and some mechanics, working on truck engines. What was unusual, for such a typical Cubano, was that his four children—three boys, and a girl—all were believed to reside in Miami, Florida, which explained where the money must come from for the nice pad. They had all made it safely to the American coast, on four separate trips, leaving him in Habana with one grandson to look after, who in turn would look after him.

Samuel had no prior arrests, neither did the grandson, now twenty-four years old and sharing the same name. But there was something quite strange to Raul—a rooftop apartment, openly flaunting an unregistered casa particular operation. Why even have one? The market of foreign visitors willing to take the risk of staying at an off-the-books place, and having their trip plans compromised, their belongings unapologetically combed through, could not be very substantial. And with such a great location, and the relatively easy hygiene and utility requirements to actually be certified, there seemed no logical reason to avoid it. Unless the risk of little business was more appealing to Samuel than the requirement of quarterly inspections. That's it, thought Raul. Samuel does not need the money, he does not want the uniformed hassle. He opens up his place to others, once in a while, as a favor. But a favor to whom? To Lazaro? To a likable young American?

To whom?

* * * *

Old Samuel sat in the center of the couch, watching the international news on the television. Sandra sat to his right, her knees pulled up to her chest, her eyes big and concentrated. Gabrel watched her, standing, leaning against the wall. He could almost see the neurons firing in her brain, soaking in the information, the colors, the action. He had no real idea what the newscasters were saying, a montage of a report skipping from one country to the next, throughout the Caribbean, Latin America, and on to the non-Spanish-speaking world abroad. Really, in the light of the television screen, she looked even younger than she was—a school girl more amazed by the technology than the reports. In her world, Gabrel reasoned, these events floated far out on the periphery. They had no impact she could see, and life for her had probably been so consistent, always consistent, there was little logic in thinking any new developments very important. One of the reasons he had come here was to discover, in an era of satellites and internet connections, how formidable the walls to the fortress could really still be. In Sandra's expression he read a version of the answer.

As enchanting an exercise as it was to play voyeur from a few feet away, and as amicable as Old Samuel seemed, Sourdough wanted to go to his room, and he wanted Sandra to go with him. It was another unusual situation, far more complicated in his mind than in actuality. There were no secrets among them, just his own awkward sense of propriety supporting his reservations. He was paying for the room. He was paying for the room not just for the view, but because Sandra could stay—a complex reality in itself, which he was now finally comprehending. Old Samuel understood his tenant, understood Sandra's role as the tenant's mistress, and saw it as nothing short of perfectly fine. He was just watching the news, being a polite host, waiting for his guest to retire so he could do the same. But his guest was embarrassed to tell his mistress that it was time to justify her board.

And she, the onus on him, was the most relaxed of the three; watching the show, a welcome end to the day. She knew that Lazaro was a little upset, but since he definitely was not thinking about her at the moment, she did not see a reason to think about him.

She knew he'd be back in the morning, with more suggestions and plans and ideas.

Day 5

Raul followed from the opposite side of the street. One good thing about the American operative was that he could be spotted in almost any crowd. The white skin and sandy brown hair were like beacons on a clear night—no mistaking him for Cubano. And when it came to areas like Habana Viejo, areas where Germans, Italians, and a lot of Canadians were actively taking photos and happily paying for overpriced drinks, it was the scruffy, unshaven face, and the faded cargo shorts with the frayed bottoms, always a string or two dangling, that set him apart. Not to mention the small black bag, draped over a shoulder, from which he often pulled out a camera of his own, or that notebook, or a thick guidebook, consulting a map. With time, Raul noticed that the American only stopped to get out the camera, or the guidebook, in the tourism areas, and even there seemed a bit more self-conscious about it than most travelers. When he was at a café frequented by locals, or on a street outside of Viejo, the only object he would ever pull out was the notebook, and always for a solid ten minutes of writing, broken by periods of looking around, watching the locals go about their daily life.

He was on his way toward Viejo today, but not to the restaurants or churches. He stopped at the old Presidential Palace, now the Museo da la Revolucion. Instead of going straight inside, the American circled the property, lingering around the back, where the great vessel Granma was the centerpiece of an outdoor display including notable military vehicles from different eras, and a few noteworthy pieces of U.S. property, too. Soldiers on foot guarded the premises, and signs in major languages explained clearly that there was to be no loitering. This was not so much from security concerns as wanting the foreigners to pay the museum entrance fee if they wanted to see the artifacts. But the phrasing on the signs, and the noticeable military presence, left many visitors fearful of strolling by too slowly, let alone stopping to re-tie a shoe.

Raul watched from afar as the American did his walk around, stopping three times, hands in pockets, totally relaxed, almost cocky, almost daring one of the soldiers to approach and make a big deal of it. Exactly what Raul did not want to see, and he breathed a sigh of relief each time the American turned, and continued. When he entered the front of the museum, through the grand white doors of the old mansion, Raul took a seat on a nearby bench. There was only one way in and out, and no need to know which exhibits the operative found most interesting. It was also a very high-visibility place, with security cameras that could be checked later, if necessary, as well as many foreigners around, with their digital cameras and observant eyes. It would be a terrible place for an altercation or incident of any kind, because there was no reasonable way to prevent the tourists from rapidly spreading their versions worldwide. Raul would wait, and ponder the morning's new, dangerous guidance.

They directed him to "engage the target". Raul understood the terminology; a big difference between "engage", "confront", and "eliminate". Someone with a higher salary than his, someone who actually worked out of an office, had decided to go on the offensive. Raul wondered what from his reports would have led them to change the strategy. Was it something he wrote, or something he left out? If he was not drawing a full portrait of the situation, they might be anxious for more detail. If he was providing information that supported some theory of theirs, or validated an expectation he did not know about, that might have pushed them to this reaction. Then there was also the outside chance Raul was not the only set of eyes keeping tabs on the situation. This was what worried him most—he knew his gambling left him exposed, and maybe it was hoping against hope to think that would go unnoticed, to assume they were leaving the fate of their plans entirely in his rusty hands.

Whatever the case, Raul was told to "engage". Engagement meant making his presence known to the operative, then reporting the reaction—a dangerous move. You did not just walk up to a foreign agent, tap them on the shoulder, and passively inform them that, if they had not noticed, you were monitoring their every move, background checking every waiter, cashier, and taxi driver they interacted with, and you were not just doing it for fun. From his experience, the main reason Higher would move to engage was either they were not sure of the target's intentions, or they were very, very sure of the intentions, but not sure of their conviction. Meaning, could Raul manage to have the entire job aborted—whatever that job was—at the first sign that their cover was compromised? Or was the mission so high a priority that such a realization would be met with furiously violent resistance?

Raul remembered the last time he had been directed to "Engage". Fernando reacted to the situation like a man sentenced to death who had been anticipating the verdict for quite some time, and seemed almost relieved that the waiting was over. That was back in the days when they needed each other alive, and his managers were confident enough in their deceptive security system to view the known evil as an acceptable risk, and a preferred option to new shadows. Now that his old friend seemed sidelined, looking back, Raul thought they were lucky the calm stalemate lasted as long as it did.

* * * *

Gabrel slid his bag across the counter, accepting the little piece of tin with a number 6 scratched into it, and walking up the stairs. There were no cameras or bags allowed in the museum, as though the artifacts on display were enclosed in temperature-controlled cases and sensitive to the light of a flash. More likely, he suspected, a precaution in line with the excess security. It was as though the museum did not expect school children on field trips, or local youths wanting to re-trace the recent history; it was a for-profit system geared for sapping revenue from passport carriers. Truth be told, he did not mind paying. It was worth getting to hear their side of things.

There were many small rooms, a reminder that the place had been built to be lived in, not to display old newspaper clippings and basic soldiering equipment, metal canteens and portable field radios. The walls were lined with display cases, photos and rosters and maps with military graphics set down in a long timeline, winding like a snake from one room into the next. Middle-aged women in modest blue vests and skirts sat in chairs, one per display, fanning themselves with brochures and overseeing the steady flow of the visitors. They did not say anything or return eye contact—but pointed the way to keep passersby on pace, in the appropriate direction. Gabrel had accidentally entered the exhibit covering the 1970's straight across the hall from the 1940's, and was efficiently re-directed. It seemed important to learn everything in order, for genuine clarity.

But he already knew most of the basics, and lingered longest at the display cases with the photos of the martyrs, especially the leaders of the underground movements in Habana and Santiago; their piece in the process did not make news off of the island. They were mostly forgotten. Gabrel spent a long time studying the old glass Pepsi bottles, with the explanations of how the Molotov Cocktails were made, what they were utilized for. He studied every detail of the radio equipment used, from the countryside, to counter government propaganda with flavor-filled slices of their own, gradually digging deeper and deeper into the thoughts of the island's listeners.

There were a great deal of newspaper clippings, or copies of them, tacked very simply into corkboard, as if the curator of the museum was a teenager decorating their bedroom. The clippings focused a lot on the U.S.—Cuban relations, with little blurbs presented in both Spanish and English, explaining detail by detail the events, the "triumphs over Imperialism", which led to to the current situation. Gabrel tried to absorb the information objectively, and almost wanted to give the authors of the explanations the benefit of the doubt. He kept from forming an opinion by regularly reminding himself that "it doesn't matter what you think". Still, the ultimate goal was to have an opinion, once a sufficient pile of input was processed. Input from all parties.

Gabrel passed through the three floors of exhibits. The first was dedicated to past heroes, particularly Jose Marti. The second, to the landing, and the battles, and the stormy first decade, the tiny nation's weighty role in the tumultuous Cold War events. The third floor canonized Che and Camillo, but Gabrel had not come to the museum to learn about them—he intended to search closer to the sources of their legends, later. On his way back downstairs, and out to the equipment and vehicle displays, he walked along a wing that did not seem an official part of the museum layout, but is wasn't off limits, either. It held life-size caricature depictions of US presidents and "the traitors", their Central American allies. Others might have stopped, amused or shocked or insulted. But Gabrel did not care much for bloated propaganda. The images cheapened the atmosphere.

Walking out onto the palace grounds, around the eternal flame, the tattered spy plane fuselage, the flame-throwing farm tractor, he paid little attention to the weapon-wielding soldiers symbolically holding their posts. What began to distract Sourdough's attention away from the freshly-painted yacht, what made him start to think about leaving, was the man that was watching him, arms folded, leaning against the wall of the main building. He was no soldier, no groundskeeper or museum employee. He did not look like a tourist, but a local, and if he had come to view the artifacts, he would be casually doing just that, instead of so obviously staring at Gabrel. There was no way back into the building without walking past him. And there was no rational reason to feel threatened in such surroundings, so Sourdough did, feeling the heavy stare stick to him as he passed. The man stunk of cigarettes, and did not pursue him into the building.

Moving directly to the receptionist counter, he offered the small tin number in exchange for his bag. The woman, in her modest blue outfit, handed it to him, but held on for a moment, long enough for him to give her a confused "Why are you still holding on?" look, long enough for her to answer with an honest, blank gaze. She let go, which was when he noticed it had a piece of paper—a piece that looked as though it had been torn in a rush from his own notebook—attached with a safety pin to the outer top of the bag, near the zipper teeth.

Gabrel read the note on his way to the door, feeling his nerve try to escape out of the skin on his arms.

"I can help."

He paused, started to turn, changed his mind, and left the building, removing the note from its place, sliding the paper into his pocket, heading toward the edge of Habana Viejo, and the bar he was starting to think of as his safe zone.

From a second floor window of the museum, Fernando watched him hurry off. From a bench near the entrance, looking up at the window, Raul wondered what the hell had just happened, so quickly, so much sooner than he had expected. Fernando turned his head, looked down at him, and waved.

* * * *

The Bar Monserrate had many things going its way, at least by Gabrel's standards. The location, on the edge of Habana Viejo, where the district brushed up against Habana Centro, meant the bulk of business came from chalky-skinned tourists, but that the room was not so heavily scrutinized by policia to stop a decent balance of locals from sprinkling into the crowd. The laid-back style stood in complimentary contrast to the tourism vacuum next door, an over the top restaurant bar with loud signs you could not help notice, a reputation built on exaggerated legend, unpenetrably dark, tinted glass windows that forced the curious to either enter and discover the truth, or move on and never quite know. They also had an overrated rum and grapefruit house cocktail, something Sourdough honestly wanted to sample, but not if it meant condoning the rest of the place's obnoxiousness.

By contrast to such stuffiness, Monserrate had no windows at all. It reminded Gabrel of an American Old West saloon, with a swinging gate entrance carved from wood, similar carvings stretching around the sides that faced the sidewalks, so the Son music floated uninhibited into the street, the rhythm of the voice and the drums drowning out even the loudest of the oversized trucks. The bow-tied meseros were quick with the orders, the band did not hassle for tips, and, a miracle, instead of music videos on the television propped up above the far corner of the bar, they were showing the afternoon's local baseball game.

He only gave the note a few minutes of concern. The hustler factor in the city was more of an annoyance than he originally thought, on the first day, when it seemed that a steady straight-ahead stare and no reaction to their hisses and simple English phrases was sufficient enough a repellent. But Lazaro was getting under his skin, the likelihood of another visit, another suggestion of Gabrel financially sponsoring a grand party of three or four or who knows how many at a disco, spoiled every moment he spent in the penthouse apartment, lying with Sandra or reflecting on the patio.

That meant the streets were becoming the safe haven, the break from anxiety that his lodging should be providing. This only multiplied his frustration every time an alley simpleton whispered "Cigaro" or braved a few steps in stride, offering "You want cigar? You want girl?" He was beginning to feel fully constricted, surrounded—the streets, the apartment, and now, he had been approached inside a museum, apparently with museum employee cooperation, his bag violated, the legitimacy of the place disrespected.

Gabrel took another sip of the drink, turning his attention to the band. There were two singers, a smooth man in his late forties, and a woman with a tight body, but also at least thirty. Sometimes they sang lyrics, but mostly the voices were instruments, hitting notes to blend into the blanket of sound produced by the guitar, and the drums, and the bass. Very nice, how they danced to their own music, eyes closed or looking off at nothing special, their minds too in synch with the song to bother working the room with winks and smiles, the way they might if they were more interested in business than in art. Gabrel realized, again, and not for the last time, how easily a traveler could slip into stereotypes, how conveniently quick judgments, sweeping generalizations and on the spot declarations could produce opinions about a place, and a culture, as unfair and incomplete as the articles in the Party newspaper.

Lazaro had pushed him to focus on the negative, and he needed a way to regroup, to enjoy the trip and absorb details more objectively. Sandra could be the catalyst for change. It was nice to know she was waiting, right now, on Old Samuel's couch. It sucked that she could not go out with him, reasons again throwing him into thoughts of disgust, not just with the government, but the rotten, single-minded thinking of the populace. But to leave the city now was too much like a retreat. He still felt safe, and if not in control, at least on equal ground with the streetwise old boxer.

The song was over, and the band took a short break to refresh. A half-shell tray began to subtly make its way around the wood tables. Gabrel reached into his pocket to pull out a bill, but instead his fingers found the little note. "I can help." The alcohol in the drink stimulated his imagination, and there was no denying something beyond the ordinary about a message written in English. And the boldness of the operation, using the paper from his bag, in a building not just with every corner under videotaped surveillance, but the watchful eyes of employees who probably needed the salary too much to risk it on a hustler pushing low-quality cigars. A part of him wanted to go back, to confront the man, to make up for his startled escape. Another mojito and he probably would.

As for the museum, it required no more of his time. Interesting, the tone of the exhibits, in line with the theme of the many billboards and posters around town, as though the book was not closed, the final chapter not written, because the struggle would go on, against the great enemy, and all of the great enemy's allies, and all of the allies' allies.

The museum had left out one element, Gabrel thought as he ordered another drink. Whoever was fighting the battles at least had an inkling, based on all the policia on patrol, where the most difficult opposition in the final segment would come from. The details of that encounter, depending on the results, might require a new floor of displays, or just one match to burn the whole palace down.

* * * *

"I can have you arrested."

"I'd make a lot of noise, trapped in a box like that."

"You're a lot more afraid of them than you are of us. That's a huge mis-estimation, Fernando."

"Maybe we both only act because we fear our masters more. Did you ever think of that?"

"If someone else finds out you are interfering, they may have you killed. If they find out I knew about, I could end up dead with you. That's a pretty tough position for you to put me in."

"You assume I'm just taking initiative for self-preservation."

"What I assume is that you recognize, if you are cooperating with that agent, and I find out you have misled me, I won't need my superiors to tell me what to do."

It was Fernando's turn to walk away. He could sense new anxiety and impatience in his old friend, a man who knew a lot of dirty jokes, and was better at chess than crossword puzzles or billiards. Their relationship had circled; the line had blurred, then altogether disappeared, and now it was solid again, as nonnegotiable and stone serious as the day they first met. The big difference, from the old days, was how each man felt cock-sure he could read the other's bluff, and anticipate their next move. Ultimately, Raul viewed him as a nuisance, not a danger.

Fernando believed the secret to winning the round might be treating Raul like as much of a daunting mystery as the young traveler whose arrival sparked this confrontation. He got a rush from his move in the museum, and had gone from struggling to sleep last night to now looking forward to whatever happened next. Raul was a little bit wrong. It was not his master Fernando most feared.

✳   ✳   ✳   ✳

Sandra admired herself in the vanity mirror on top of the bedroom dresser. Her hair was wrapped in a towel, like an African turban atop her head. She thought it would be funny, that he would like it, if she slipped into the bright red and orange tie-dye t-shirt he wore out on his walk, before he noticed, flipping through pages of the guidebook. The shirt fit perfectly, ending a few centimeters below her genital area, her long, smooth black legs taking over from there. By now he realized she was out of the shower, and he turned on his camera for a shot.

She liked the camera very much, an easy model to use, automatically adjusting to the light, focusing, and then just a turn of a knob to look at the photo result. She liked seeing herself—the most flattering images she had ever seen, the Americano very good at finding the right angle, framing her perfectly whether she was by the mirror, on the patio, or in the shower, where she looked best, and she knew it. Sandra also enjoyed viewing the photos of the day, and from his other long walks, to the cafes and bars, along the coast, and of the statues and buildings she passed by all the time, but never thought to pause and check out.

She liked the travel book, too. It was thick enough to be an encyclopedia, the kind you might keep on your shelf, but not something to carry around all day. Just another detail that made the Americano crazier than most guys she had known. The book did not just cover the city, but all of Cuba, with full-page color photos identifying the must-see places, the must-do things, all the way to Santiago, where an aunt of hers lived, and where she used to spend summer vacation from school. Sourdough did not seem to mind her looking through it, and Sandra did not mind that she could not read the writing. Many things she recognized, but did not bother trying to explain. Some of the locales she had been to many times; they looked new, fresh, somehow different on the glossy pages. He seemed to know what he wanted to see. He seemed to know at least as much as she did about the place she lived all her life.

Gabrel bought some cans of beer from a small store on his way back to the apartment, had placed them in the room's micro-fridge, and now took one out to drink. Little tendencies of his helped Sandra forget how restless, and a little dirty, she felt waiting all day, while he roamed. Little tendencies, like how much he enjoyed her wearing his shirt, or taking photos just to hand her the camera, and watch her look them over. And that he would rather open one can of beer, and pass it back and forth between them, and go through all four cans this way, then be concerned about sharing, or neurotic in that way.

These details helped, but failed to completely erase the restlessness, wondering who he might be meeting, not out of jealousy, but fear of a sudden replacement; Sourdough walking out of that elevator with a prettier, or friskier, or lighter-skinned girl on his arm. This was the concern that led Lazaro to tell her to stay where she was, no errands home or on some other business. What Sourdough did on his walks was out of her control, but if he came back early, wanting attention, finding an empty apartment and going back out hunting company, well, that was a scenario Lazaro did not permit.

The details also failed to completely erase the layer of dirtiness Sandra was not used to. Her experiences were very much the opposite of the Americano's; he had traveled the world to encounter it, but the world had come looking for Sandra. He came, like the rest. The approach, the openness, made him different. Sourdough seemed to believe the more he revealed himself to her, the more she would, to him. This made her think about how much easier and less stressful dishonest relations could be. It also made her think about how young, and attractive, and intelligent he was. And Sandra did not want to think too long about that.

* * * *

Most of the hotels in Habana were off-limits, a government policy forbidding citizens from taking the space reserved for well-paying visitors. Also, another technique to deter prostitution. Hotels did not dare challenge the law, and most of their patrons, thirsty for a good time as they might be, primarily wanted to see the sights, buy a few souvenirs, and avoid the policia at all costs. Those who could not subdue their desires were willing to venture into the darkest alleys, where the risks were worth the gain.

Lazaro sat in the corner, the same position as that first night with the Americano, who said his name was Gabrel, in the bar room of the Hotel Lincoln. If the hotel were located closer to Habana Viejo, it would do the kind of business, and feel the kind of heat, to be as closed to Lazaro as all the "proper" places. But in the Centro, a district past its prime, overcrowded with unemployed stand-arounds, dirty, and desperate for the old days when its equidistant proximity to the Malecon and Viejo, and the bustling draw of a thriving Chinatown, brought internationals with fat wallets to the spot, these were days for a survival mentality. Lazaro knew every doorman, every security guard, every shift manager at the hotel. He was waiting for Marcella, upstairs in room 218, and he was watching more Shakira on the TV in the otherwise empty bar.

He recognized Raul as soon as the aging man glided into the room. They did not have many years difference between them, and probably crossed paths several times without realizing this day would come. Lazaro despised policia; especially the kind that enjoyed the harassment, did it for the thrill, the power rush, never admitting to themselves what a sad pawn they were, what a foolish string puppet they had become. Some of them knew the score, saw themselves as protectors of the people, instead of enforcers of the government, and did their best to balance the law and the needs. Others were like this one, holding a grudge for no reason, or disciples to the ideology; or, even worse, morons.

Raul sensed the resentment, but he sat down anyway. If he could not engage the operative, he could push Lazaro's buttons, gauge the reaction, go from there. The little man knew how to wear defiance on his face—the confidence of letting Raul know, before he opened his mouth, that this would not be the first time someone tried to strong-arm him. Men like Lazaro had learned along the way not to care for anything so greatly they might need to sacrifice their values to preserve or hold onto it. Leveraging, and blackmail, were games he did not play passively.

That very pride in being unshakable, and the fact, ultimately, Lazaro was bluffing, were what Raul banked this gamble on. Colorful as his boasts to friends might sound, the fighter was getting old, and the grind of working a customer, the haggling that sometimes meant accepting almost nothing to avoid a totally wasted night, and the process of handling and recruiting the young girls, dealing with pregnancies and sickness, infections and disease, had to be wearing him out. He was nearing the age when the notion of time in prison also could easily mean dying there, among emotionless strangers and bastards, last days spent in tough labor instead of in an air-conditioned hotel bar. Either Lazaro's hardened defiance was a convincing bluff, or he despised the system so much, the hatred interfered with his hustler logic. Raul did not believe a man who spent his days in such self-serving ways had a level of dignity so powerful.

Lazaro meant to begin on the offensive, to run this rat off his turf, back to his pitiful station and pathetic underlings. But Raul broke his rhythm right away.

"I want to talk to you about your American friend. He's more of a danger to you than am I." It was a guess, that either Lazaro was so low on the totem pole he did not know what was really going on, or he was entirely outside of the loop. The truth was, aside from the forty on the first night, the Americano had not given Sandra any more money, as if she was present for free, or it was okay to run up a bill. That was what Lazaro had been considering, the risk of an early confrontation, when Raul walked into the bar.

Raul continued, pushing his momentum. "You see I am not wearing a uniform, yet you know me from the station. Have you seen me before? Have I messed with you before? Think about it, Lazaro. Think about what you are risking. If you don't help me, you are siding with him. And I represent a very powerful hand."

Lazaro stayed quiet, but he was listening. Ever since he was a young teenager, and he first learned how to fight in the street, he had developed a habit of sizing up every man he encountered, no matter how much older or younger they were. Before he could move on to business, he developed a strategy in his mind. If they were bigger, they were probably slower. If they were smaller, he would have the reach advantage. The younger ones likely did not know how to fight, it was becoming a lost art. The older ones might put up a scratchy resistance at first, but if he hung in there, exchanging blows, eventually they would fade.

This opponent, with the strong words, the things he left out as meaningful as the hints he included, had not taken much care of his body. He seemed smart, the type to bring a sophisticated strategy, but also the kind so nervous about his stamina, he needed to lunge for a quick knockout. Lazaro would just let him keep swinging, keep absorbing the hits, until the rumbler exhausted his arsenal.

Day 6

To get from the penthouse apartment to la Plaza de la Revolucion, Gabrel needed to follow the map from the guidebook through a section of the city fresh to him. He set out early, after another good desayuno whipped up by Old Samuel; an egg, plenty of mango and banana, bread, butter, orange juice and café con leche, the Cuban latte that was the pivotal joint in Gabrel's mornings. Aside from the bread, normally filled with tiny, black ants, fighting for their own portion of breakfast, no sickness or bad taste to the meal. Sandra ate hers quietly, knowing Sourdough would soon head for the door. The good news was his plan for the day, starting early to return early, as Lazaro had ensured him Sandra could go to the baseball stadium for tonight's game, set on the outskirts of the city, where the rules of conduct were not in force. He looked forward to taking her out, and to being somewhere closer to the intimate lives of the locals.

Gabrel tore the map from the guidebook, something he regretted not doing sooner, now easily carried in his pocket, or his palm, not drawing so much attention to him, not requiring so heavy a load. Young Samuel suggested he take a taxi, but the route had some notables along the way. He would pass the University, and on his return, swing by the Parque de Lennon, an odd homage to a rock star that he had to see to believe.

Gabrel wanted to cover as much ground as he could, since he also had decided to leave the next day. He would not tell Sandra, or Old Samuel, until the morning, hoping to slip out before Lazaro could track him down and try to coerce him into another ploy. It had been hard to sell the idea of just Sandra and he at the ball game, no Lazaro, and Gabrel could tell the only reason the old boxer consented was a belief it was part of a negotiation, or exchange, and that Sourdough would have to say "yes" to something at a later date, to bring them back to an even keel.

On his way to the Plaza, he passed the University, students dressing and acting as college students do all over the world. They lived only a few miles from Sandra, but they lived in a different world. He also passed a grand garden, a small zoo, and had gone slightly off-course before seeing the signs, following them, and finding himself alone in a vast, concrete parking lot, in front of a magnificent tower, with a speaking platform on the top. Here, men had stood, witnessing history, and wondering how it would affect them. Here, some had cheered and rallied with sincere optimism, and some, year by year, cheered and rallied out of habit, and out of a reluctance to consider the alternatives. There were still some who cheered out of pride, and resentment to certain opposing possibilities. But now, at this moment, Gabrel stood alone. There was no scheduled rally, and he considered the symbolism of his solo occupation of the square.

* * * *

Sandra sat on the couch, watching the variety show with more involved attention than the show was probably used to receiving. She leaned forward, her forearms on her knees, the remote control between her two hands. Young Samuel lounged on the chair next to the couch. He had a few hours before work, to relax and maybe do a little reading.

This was not the first time he met Sandra, but they never were alone in a room before; never in a situation that called for polite, casual conversation. He was only a few years ahead of her, so there was that natural familiarity, that commonness of seeing and experiencing big picture events as two parts of the same generation, of dealing with and caring for relatives of the same age, who also, though they did not know each other, shared their own respective bonds.

Young Samuel's job in the hospital required maturity, an ability to remain calm and make clear decisions in situations far more stressful than this. He knew that if he kept up his studies, finished the night classes, and did not do anything stupid, a good career, and a life of reasonable comfort, waited only a few years away. His grandfather told him a young man needed challenging goals, mountains to climb, rivers to cross. Without these, young men sunk into stasis, the potential of their skills dulled, their talents traded in for efforts toward easier payoffs. He knew the pressure, the constant reminders, was a part of Old Samuel's plan to keep him moving, and reaching, until he woke up one day, entirely out of the muck.

Young Samuel knew a lot of girls. He knew a lot of pretty, fun-loving, intelligent girls, who liked to dance and to fool around with boys, and who wanted someday to settle down, raise a man's children, and spend a lifetime loving him. He appreciated his good fortune, to have the friends he had, to know the girls he knew. But he did not know, as a friend, or anything else, any girls like Sandra. At this moment, giggling at the shenanigans of the players on the show, she was just as carefree as the rest of them. He admired her for it, wondered, as honest young men do, if he had developed, in his relatively healthy life, the intestinal fortitude to handle reality as well as this girl did. Maybe reality depressed him more than it bothered her. If so, he reasoned, all the more impressive, and attractive; her cheery disposition.

* * * *

Lazaro popped out of the elevator exactly on time—seven o'clock, with a warm smile and the confident nod of a man whose mind had other things on it. Gabrel anticipated another awkward conversation, having to remind, and re-negotiate the terms for the evening. Lazaro had assured him Sandra could go to the stadium, that the two of them could travel, by taxi, no problem, and that it would in fact be two, not three, snuggling in the back seat. To Sourdough's surprise, there was no new resistance. Lazaro patted him on the shoulder, almost eager to move them along.

"Hey man, I have taxi, good man, friend of mine, is no problem. You ready?"

The air carried some friction, since Sourdough had only really returned a half-hour before, and did not bring any food, meaning Sandra was hungry, and not yet willing to forgive him for abandoning her for the maximum time. In her whole life, she had never been to one of the baseball games, and tonight she worried she was going with someone who would be more focused on the field than on her, as he seemed more focused on the statues and stories of the streets of the city than on her, until time for bed. It had only taken a few days for her to soften to the comforts of the penthouse, and forget about things like trying to sell stolen watches. The idle hours fed her thoughts, encouraging her resentment of being treated like a pet.

On the way down the lift, Lazaro explained that they would need to do a staggered exit, just to be safe, but that everything was taken care of with the driver. The taxi waited outside of the building, straight out the door. For reasons Gabrel did not understand, but figured he'd go along with, Lazaro would get into the taxi, with Sandra. Gabrel would exit the building, turn right, and walk to the end of the sidewalk, to the corner. The taxi would pull forward the half-block, Lazaro would get out, Gabrel would climb in, and off they would ride to the stadium. He wanted to ask Sandra what she thought of the need for her to be constantly, publicly, with someone. But he figured his Spanish was not good enough to communicate the depth of the question, or even if it was, to comprehend the depth of her answer. He obeyed the direction robotically, only a little worried Lazaro would stay in the cab, just another thing that would piss him off, but the old boxer held up his end, the process followed like clockwork, and in a few quick moments they were out of the Centro, on a street, in a direction new to Gabrel, which was right in line with what he wanted. Sandra slid her hip against his in the backseat, and seemed inspired, maybe by the fresh air and almost normal, almost date-like feel of the event, to at least momentarily forgive him.

* * * *

Raul waved down the next taxi he saw. It was an old classic, a Chevy, at least the shell of it was, and after all these years still holding some shine on the chrome fender.

"Take me to the stadium."

"Gladly, I was heading that way, myself."

Raul looked up at the first sound of the voice to see Fernando, smiling at him in the rearview mirror, pulling back out into traffic. "I recommend you lock your door, senor, I am told this is a dangerous area."

"If you don't take me to the stadium, I might reach up there and cut your throat."

Fernando laughed, a full, hearty, sober laugh. "Then we might miss the first pitch. Enjoy the ride. Oh, and you don't need to pay a fare, friend. Cover my ticket, we'll call it even. Buy me a hot dog, maybe I'll even take you back afterward!"

Raul could feel the perspiration gathering in small pools in his palms. Fernando had outmaneuvered him, again, and in a way that seemed protective of the operative. Indeed, he may have to kill the old sport. "How did you know they were going to the game?"

"How did you?"

"Fernando, I'm telling you for the last time, this is going to get very serious. It's going to get very serious, tonight. I don't know what you think you're doing, or how you think this can help you, but-"

"You keep threatening me, friend, and I'll make it two hot dogs, and a cerveza. And I don't know what you plan to do, to him, or to me, but I would be thoughtful about it. Remember, I've had just as many chances to finish you. Enjoy the ride, and ask yourself why I might be holding off."

* * * *

Sandra could see the anticipation drain out of Sourdough's face as they entered the stadium and searched for their seats. The place was impressive enough of a venue, yet almost completely empty; less than twenty fans in the stands, watching the ball players from both teams stretch, playing catch, warming up for the game. Confused, Gabrel gradually realized, and managed to explain to Sandra, that the city of Habana actually hosted two baseball franchises—the powerful Industrials, and the far less capable Metros. Tonight, the Metros were playing an equally unpopular team from another part of the island. The Industrials had a game on the road, and presumably all of their fans had stayed home, to watch on television, or listen on the radio, rather than venturing out to witness a second-class team first-hand. With the option of sitting basically anywhere they wanted to, Gabrel led Sandra down behind the home dugout, with a good view of the mound and any right-handed batters.

Sandra knew only the basic principles of the game. Cuban sports belonged to the men who wasted their days arguing statistics in the parks. The only man Sandra ever had real conversations with was Lazaro, and he did not carry an interest in the league. If he talked about sports at all, it was the stories of old glories in the ring—stories she could tell, by now, in better detail than he could remember—or other side comments of modern champions, but only regarding their skill level in relation to Lazaro's, in his prime. She could feel the Americano watching her look around, at the scoreboard, at the players taking their positions in the field, as though he were waiting to witness a fireworks show.

Gabrel brought along his camera, and was already busy zooming in and tilting it at angles to frame the diamond, timing certain pitches to try to capture the batter mid-swing; a hit at the moment of impact. Gradually, and to Sandra's delight, he tired of the game, transferring his efforts to her, with stylish shots from low angles, from behind her head as she watched, cheering and laughing a little when some action caught her amusement, and some playful video—the camera could handle fifteen-second increments—of the two of them talking in Spanish, of him teaching her the American words.

"Inn-ings."

"En-engs?"

"Inn-ings."

"En—ings?"

"Bueno. Ahora, 'Bat-ter'."

"Beh-ter?"

"Si, si. Ahora-"

Fernando and Raul shared a bag of peanuts, watching the young couple flirt from far down the left field line, a safe enough distance for Sandra not to be able to make out Raul's features, or for Gabrel to notice Fernando. They were both letting their guards down a little, settling into the rhythm of the early innings, the two teams testing each other's defense, the control and speed of the pitchers holding everything together on the mound.

"What if he just wanted to see a game?" Fernando asked, tossing another shell to his feet, kicking it back, under his seat. "I guess that means a night off for everybody!"

Raul kept his eyes on the operative. The thing about a job like this, the thing he did not want to bother explaining to Fernando, who was beginning to annoy him, was that there were almost always two possible explanations, two possible answers to the question "Why?". But those explanations often carried tremendously different consequences, and degrees of consequence, if you happened to guess wrong, or guess at all. Raul was not as paranoid and out of touch as his managers and handlers sometimes seemed, with their over-cautious and psycho-curious directives. The possibility that the American had just wanted to catch a ball game was as likely as the un-ignorable chance he was just a bold tourist without any connection to or knowledge of events, whose only misstep was assuming he could fly below the radar of his home country's embargo policy without it being a big deal to the forces that clearly were not as much of a perilous threat in his mind as they were in the minds of his leaders.

A pop fly ended the third inning, and as the home team returned to their positions, the American stood, the girl staying in her seat, clicking through the photos in the camera as he walked to the end of the aisle and disappeared down the ramp, into the bowels of the stadium where the restrooms, concessions, and souvenir shops were. Raul turned to Fernando. "If you stay here and keep an eye on her, I promise not to cause an international incident, and to tell you exactly what happens."

Fernando could see his old friend was trying not to give him an ultimatum. They were drinking buddies before, maybe they could be again sometime. He nodded, Raul rose, and hurried off.

As he rushed around, hoping he wasn't too late, Raul continued to think about the disproportionately different risks. If this American was the flavor of operative his managers and handlers had been pinpointing and neutralizing for decades, evidenced by the fact they were still the ones calling the shots, than this stadium, on a night like this, was the perfect place to meet another piece in the puzzle. Here, he could study every other fan, there were only a handful, so his meeting would not be easily compromised or eavesdropped on. The girl was the perfect excuse, and his decision to haul her so far out of town, to waste a few hours watching a boring contest, made him seem a lot more like a puppeteer than just a simple man with a weakness for easy company. Raul rounded into the right field wing of the stadium bowels, gambled, and headed toward the men's restroom. The greatest danger was not Fernando being correct, and this all being a harmless misunderstanding. The greatest danger was the operative convincing Raul this was the case.

His body constricted as he suddenly slowed, his chest tightening, something squeezing his airflow. He reached for a pillar, a vertical beam supporting the stands, steadying himself. Raul felt like he had been shot in the chest, and stabbed in his right arm, too. He did not need a doctor to know what that meant. With so many things on his mind, he had forgotten the pills on the nightstand. Raul closed his eyes, re-balanced, opened them, used his arm to shove his body weight off of the pillar, and gradually built a new head of steam.

He rounded the corner of the entrance, into the restroom, moving at a very fast clip. Raul was moving so fast because he feared he would find the place empty, then need to back track and frantically search another restroom, or hustle up the ramp to the top deck that overlooked home plate, or down another corridor he'd somehow failed to notice. He was moving so fast because he expected, if the American indeed was in the restroom, he would be in a stall, or at the open trough, taking a piss, his back to the entrance, giving Raul time to settle himself, and the opportunity to make a powerfully alarming first impression. There were a hundred ways to scare the hell out of a man, when you caught him with his pants down.

Raul was moving so fast because, he had to admit, he had so desperately rushed into an offensive posture, he'd taken his opponent for granted. Twenty years ago, this thought would have triggered him to naturally regain composure. But now the warnings came too late, dawning on him just as he entered, just as a heavy object crashed into his right temple, then another into his mouth, as he fell down to the floor. He lost consciousness for about a minute, jerking alert to the taste of warm blood, and squinting at the ache of the swollen side of his face.

Raul hastily cleaned himself up at the sink, his vision still a little blurry as he labored to a payphone, calling in a coded report through the emergency line, before returning to his stadium seat. Fernando was still there, finishing off the bag of peanuts, waiting, as he'd been told to, to inform Raul that the American and the girl were long gone, that he returned to his seat at almost the same instant Raul disappeared into the corridor, making Fernando wonder what was taking so long, a search that no doubt ended in vain. He studied Raul's throbbing head, and noticed his old chess opponent was clutching his chest with an open-palmed hand.

"You want me to take you to the hospital?"

"No."

"You want to go find them again? Probably just returning to that apartment for relations."

"Let's go, Fernando. Take me back into the city."

*   *   *   *

Comandante Barbuda massaged his forehead, struggling to read and understand the details of the typed, one-page report, just delivered, the attendants waking him as he requested, if any new updates on this particular case came in. It was always interesting to him, the way these low-ranking soldiers would so obediently, time after time, carry sensitive, secretive information from one office to another, and maintain enough discipline to subdue any curiosity about the contents. Having never been in that situation, having always been a player, it was just one more piece of evidence that there are certain kinds of people, and then there are other kinds of people. The trick of a good system was placement; you never want to ask someone to perform below their abilities. Those are the kind that get restless, get curious, and cause problems. Better to have an overworked simpleton than an under-utilized brainiac. He had seen a lot of leaders fall from grace, just because they did not understand this principle.

His reading glasses were over on the table, which would require climbing into his wheelchair, or ringing the bell and having them fetched, but Barbuda did not have time for that; his attention was devoted to the memo. Holding it close to his nose, he read through it twice, a third time, before he realized he was not alone in the room. The ghost had come back, to torment him.

"My agent confirms the operative's legitimacy."

"Does he, now?"

"And his willingness to engage in violence, on top of that, in a public arena."

"Does he, now?"

"I'm going to postpone the event."

"Why not just cancel, and wave a white flag while you're at it? Postponing buys them more time. You are still the determining factor, aren't you? Aren't you still the one making the moves, forcing them to be the reactors?"

"They count on my pride overwhelming my judgment. Because they are so full of machismo, they assume it a weakness in everyone."

"I don't disagree with that."

"We tried plucking a feather from a rooster, to see how it would respond, and now we seem surprised, to find that it is a rooster. You are correct, I am the determining factor. I can postpone as long as I like. They think I am arrogant, and they think I'm nervous of running out of time. Let him wander the streets for another week, see if he can stay out of trouble. They are all professional when the job is straight forward, but most of them can't handle indefinite downtime."

"I don't disagree with that."

Day 7

Sandra lay on her side on the bed, showered and dressed, in the same pink pull-over tank top with spaghetti straps and light blue denim jeans she wore to the baseball game last night. She watched as Sourdough gathered the few items he had spread around the room, t-shirts, papers, the bracelets and the watch, packing his black back pack, forcing everything in and struggling to close the zipper. She reached for his notebook, and the pen, turned to a blank page near the back, and started writing a message in Spanish.

She could tell all night he had something on his mind. Even though she managed to sleep soundly, she could tell, all night, that he was awake, thinking, shifting his weight around, looking for a position that might relax him a bit. They woke as they had every morning, after showers to the living room, where Old Samuel waited to prepare another breakfast. The old man, like Lazaro, did not miss the sunrise. Sandra found the detail endeared her to him, though she knew she would never be that kind.

It was during the meal, as he refilled his coffee, that the Americano announced he was leaving, that morning, explaining that he wanted to see the rest of the island now, instead of waiting, and trying to fit too many things into the tail end of his trip. He spoke a little with Old Samuel about the bus schedule, the frequency of departures to Santa Clara. They spoke of his bill, which he was eager and ready to pay on the spot, the money brought to the table for that very purpose, in his pocket. Sandra noticed that Sourdough had more of an appetite than usual. She was quickly losing her own, listening to him describe the ball game to Old Samuel, comparing it to contests in the states, transitioning away from his announcement as though it were expected, and as though all parties would be happy to hear he was going forth into another adventure.

Writing the letter in the notebook felt like the easiest outlet of her emotions Sandra had ever been able to do, or wanted to, comforted by the fact Sourdough would not really be able to read it, not really grasp the deep sincerity. She knew from watching other people on the streets, how a woman especially trembles at the thought of baring her feelings, of leaving herself wide-open to rejection. Writing the letter felt very surreal, a comforting exercise made possible due to the language barrier.

By the time she finished, he was waiting, patiently watching, that curious, amused expression back on his face. She asked when he would return to Habana, and the Americano replied with a very non-committal "quatro dias, cinco dias, no sey". He leaned in to kiss her, but she pulled up her hands in a universal gesture even he could understand; pointing her index fingers toward the center, so they met at the tips, forming a bridge between the two fists. Then she let the fingers fall; the bridge suffering an irreparable collapse.

She accommodated his last request, for her to use the camera she now understood so well, to snap a photo of him with Old Samuel, the two standing out in the sun, on the patio, with the sea a distant background. Sourdough gave the old man a hearty handshake and hug, then he and Sandra stepped into the lift, taking it to the first floor. Her face reassumed her trademark, stoic, expressionless gaze. Gabrel had worried she would be emotional, anticipated the good-bye being tough on the girl. Instead, he could see, she did not struggle to fight back any tears, or have the strain of angst and uncertainty in her eyes. Sandra looked, frankly, bored. It made him want to hug her, to give her another kiss, to beg her to beg him to stay, but that round of possibility obviously was over. Without another glance she stepped out of the elevator, out the main door of the building, turning left, toward the boxer's apartment.

* * * *

Gabrel took a roundabout route from Old Samuel's to the Capitolo. He had plenty of time to get there, to get from there to the bus terminal, and his legs and feet could handle the extra mileage if it meant avoiding an accidental run-in with Lazaro. He felt a little more conspicuous with the bulging pack on, the weight leaning him into a slightly forward tilt. Sometimes walking too far like this, with this pack, the strain of the straps around the shoulders limited blood circulation to his arms, and he would need to take a break, or shift the load, to keep his fingers and hands from tingling and going numb. But that was on long walks, mountain hikes; just a sidebar thought this morning.

No trouble reaching the taxi stand, behind the Capitolo, next to the high-end hotel, and also near the Parque Central, where the fateful meeting with Sandra, the watch, steered him into the actions of the past few days. That was the thing about traveling whimsically, open-endedly; once you bit on a tangent, once you committed to an exploration, you eliminated other possible tangents, different or opposing interpretations of the culture, from your field of vision. Gabrel knew he was leaving Habana today for several reasons. But taking at least a break from Lazaro and Sandra, enjoyable and easy as it had been, was a necessary part of the overall process. The bothersome aspect was how much better Sandra understood this than he did.

Gabrel approached a taxi, not one of the vintage old American monsters, or the rusty, beat-up yellow cabs, but a shiny new red one, the kind that lived off the hotel clientele. They charged more, but the price was standard, driver policies non-negotiable, the sort of safe option senior citizens in plaid shorts and wool socks went for. Gabrel just did not want to haggle, or have to scratch and claw in Spanish to avoid getting taken advantage of this morning. He wanted an easy ride, his mind left open for reflection.

* * * *

She knew Lazaro was going to be angry, that was why she went to his apartment first, and not finding him there, went to the Hotel Lincoln, instead of going home and taking a nap. She expected harsh words, insults, at the least, for letting the Americano disappear without even asking, or, as Lazaro would expect, calling him, stalling, giving him a chance to make it over there to talk things over, work out a fair deal.

But he was more than upset, taking the news with a loud exhale, as if someone had just rabbit-punched him. The pain started to form in his gut the second she walked through the door, into the bar—alone, with her extra clothes tucked under an arm. Sandra did not really have to say anything, not to a man with a mind like Lazaro's. He left her there, sitting at the table, rushing outside with his mobile phone, making a call—she thought she could hear him say "Samuel", ending the call, dialing urgently, making another. He disappeared down the block, returned just as quickly, sitting across from her in silence, smoking his cigarette and staring at the ashtray. When he finally spoke, Lazaro used the tone of voice usually reserved for competitors, policia, and girls he was ending his business with.

"He told you he would return?"

"Yes."

"You believe him?" Lazaro never asked Sandra her opinion, but now he was looking straight at her, very serious, as though he actually cared how she would respond. The possibility of disappointing him, or being wrong, terrified her.

"I don't know."

"I do." Lazaro gave her his friend-to-the-world smile, the twinkle back in his eyes. Of course he knew, he always knew. Just like he knew how to bring up her spirits, after she'd failed him so badly. Lazaro crushed out the rest of the cigarette, pulling a fresh one from the pack and lighting it up. He was looking at the ashtray again, planning.

* * * *

Raul watched from the passenger seat as Fernando shifted the beast into gear, pulling out of the parking lot at the zoo, across the street from the bus terminal. They had arrived in time, a few minutes before the autobus opened for boarding and loading. They could see the American, ticket in hand, pack on his back, climbing the stairs and disappearing behind the curtains on the blue whale. The sign in the window had read "Habana" on its way in, but was now replaced with "Santa Clara/Santiago" as the long vehicle swung out onto the road, heading East.

Fernando turned to Raul, smiling and nodding toward the car radio. "Why don't you find us some good road music, hermano?"

* * * *

Raul's head was still throbbing, the vibrations of the car on questionable shock absorbers not helping one bit. They had been driving most of the day, and would have easily caught the bus if not for the legal obligation to pick up hitchhikers along the road. Raul normally did not mind the rule, which not only eliminated congestion and heavy traffic on the highways, but also broke through any class barrier of "have's" and "have not's" that might allow a man with cloudy priorities to speed past workers who just wanted to get home for dinner. But they could not afford to pull over and bog the car down with burlap sacks and bananas at the cost of losing pace with the big blue cruiser.

Fernando stopped for the first man they saw, a security guard who only needed to travel five kilometers. Before dropping him off, Fernando picked up another, an old woman who would ride with them all the way to Santa Clara. She had been away from her home there for a week, helping care for a sick granddaughter on a farm. She was exactly the kind of passenger Raul wanted; going straight to their own destination, too tired and modest to ask about his business.

What the passengers prevented was a straight-forward talk with Fernando. Raul did not fully buy into his version of the American's calm return to his seat, then departure with the girl, well before he could have ambushed Raul in the restroom. It was a little obnoxious for Fernando to even suggest something like that, and then, now, so willingly assist in a continued monitoring of the dangerous operative. Higher Headquarters directed the surveillance—stressing, to Raul's satisfaction—that it should be conducted from an unexposed distance, reports submitted at every change of location and regarding any suspicious behavior. They did not offer him a vehicle, or ask how he would get around, so he did not tell them Fernando was involved. It was all still so confusing, he did not want to say anything until he could report definitively.

His plate was very full, following the American, keeping perhaps the most dangerous variable, his old chess mate, at arm's reach, and checking in with his newest associate, Lazaro, with one quick phone call a day. That negotiation turned out not to be as tough as he'd expected. The old man had his trainer license and business permit revoked ten years back. The file said he was using the locker room for illicit purposes. He just wanted to be around boxing again, and Raul promised to make it happen, as long as Lazaro kept him informed on Old Samuel's guest list, and Sandra's behavior, while the American was out of town.

Fernando pulled to the side of the road, beneath an underpass, this time to pick up a teenage boy with a live chicken securely wrapped in his arms. Raul's thoughts continued to swirl around the inevitable confrontation, and how much harder it would be on him, with every passing kilometer, as they rode further and further from Habana.

*   *   *   *

The Santa Clara terminal was on the far western edge of town. Gabrel awkwardly worked to reinsert his contact lenses in the yellow glow of the overhead light, rummaging through his bag for the book with the map of the town. He intended to walk to the center square, by all indications the popular rally point, then look for the official casa particular stickers in the windows of the houses, hopefully find a place to toss his bag before it was too late to hit a bar for a drink and sample their version of nightlife. This was no city, but it was no hick farm town, either; like the deprived, thatched roof places the bus had rolled past.

Despite the late hour, a futbol team-sized element of taxi drivers waited for the passengers at the terminal exit. They all cued in on Gabrel, and it was not until he had walked several blocks that the last driver gave up his bid. There were no tall buildings here, a very comfortable, hustler-free feel to the atmosphere, accentuated by the wagon-furgons, hauled by mules, illuminated as they trotted down the streets by old school, iron-cast lanterns dangling underneath the carriages.

The exercise of the walk helped to wake him, and achieving his objectives proved easy enough. In an hour, by his lucky Sandra watch, he had found a reasonably-priced, well-placed room, stowed his bag, tracked back to the central park, and found a seat in a lively bar on the corner of the square, choosing the place over some others because of the guitar music spilling out of it, and the seat, near the band, across from a black local who looked a hundred years old.

The old man had a toothless grin stretching from ear to ear, one of those smiles that makes the eyes disappear. He was very gradually finishing off a mojito he'd probably started when the sun was still up. Gabrel bought him another, and one for himself, energized by the night's clockwork efficiency, wanting to try out his Spanish, practiced now for days with Sandra, in a conversation with no English safety net, no one to call to, like Lazaro or Young Samuel, to interpret.

Gabrel explained his purpose; like every other tourist, there was only one reason to stop in Santa Clara. "Si, si, Che Guevara, Che Guevara, bueno!" the old man laughed, nodding with understanding and beginning a story to tease Sourdough's interest. He was wearing a faded baseball cap, no insignia, a yellowed white shirt, the collar closed, and an old black bowtie underneath a thin grey suit-jacket. He seemed like the kind of guy everybody knew, a harmless social leech who did not just tell stories, but re-lived them, feeding off of long-gone action to power him through to tomorrow. As he spoke, Gabrel realized the man was not black, as he'd first thought. His skin had become the darkest brown leather the sun could paint it; darker than the soil in the fields he had turned, tilled and ploughed so many times.

He said he was eighty-five now, pointing out to Gabrel that he was already a grown man, with a wife and two children and approaching middle-age, when the Revolution arrived in their town. "No man asks for upheaval at that age, or still entertains delusions of drastic improvement. Men of that age, as true now as it was then, can barely bring themselves to hope and pray for stability, for the energy to care for their loved ones, and the good fortune for the children to stay clear of disease." The sugar, mint, and rum were fueling him now, the music a theme song to his own movie. "My wife's brother owned that land, next to the railroad tracks. They found the bulldozer on the other side of town, chose that piece of rail for the fire positions they could get behind. It was all very exciting, and over so quickly, and nobody except maybe Che understood the importance of that little battle. Those soldiers, in those train cars, the last thing on their mind was a fight to the death, I can tell you that!"

The Battle of Santa Clara was a key ingredient in the Guevara legend. It was historically, shrewdly cast as the pivotal victory, cutting the soldiers in Santiago from their supplies and command in Habana, and serving as the one time the Argentine was calling the shots, using his guerilla mind to psychologically cripple the overwhelming number of Batista soldiers in those rail cars, who surrendered within minutes of the first shot, when the train grinded to a halt, the engineer realizing too late that the track had been demolished. Gabrel had come to see with his own eyes the layout, filter the official account through his own catalog of experiences and military knowledge. Considering that only a few days later, Batista fled the country and the Revolution was complete, he had no valid reason to question authenticity.

But listening to the old man describe how dirty, smelly, and starved Guevara's soldiers were, his own first-hand vantage point, first at the battle site, then near the army barracks where the formal surrender took place, Sourdough began to appreciate the magnitude of impact the event, and its follow-on events, had on this otherwise ordinary person. Through the years, with diligent repetition, and maybe some outside encouragement, his account of the battle had become so personalized, so polished, it was completely plausible and yet very, very unlikely. For a thirty-something fieldworker, detached from politics and beyond his years of government service, the Revolution was something that happened around him. But with time, and the magical formula of nationalist propaganda, he had transformed himself into the thing the government had convinced him he always wanted to be: a participant. Now sitting there, the band transitioning into the traditional end of night song, "Guantanamera", Gabrel accepted every detail as a sincere truth, because this was not a dishonest old man. Just an old man with treasured stories, and an enviable false sense of accomplishment.

Day 8

The morning desayuno, served by the hospitable woman in her forties, the wife and casa particular operator, tasted better, looked more sanitary than Old Samuel's offerings, but she and her father, who limped around the room hunchback, nibbling on some bread, did not compare to the feeling of breakfast with Sandra. It was difficult to think about, wonder where she was waking up, without spoiling the meal.

There were few people out this morning; Santa Clara was not a place of traffic, smog, or old beat up American dinosaur machines. Gabrel followed the town map from the book, to the site where the rail cars still stood, in piled-up disarray, with the freshly painted, famous dozer positioned on a platform, the collection of out-of-date contraptions functioning as a monument. The town had expanded since then, grown around the rail line. There were still mules hauling wagons and cobble-stoned streets, Gabrel taking some photos and moving on, up the hill to the old army barracks.

From the barracks, before heading toward the true monument, Sourdough stopped at a local cigar factory. He bought a four-pack of Romeo y Juliettas, at the recommendation of the shop owner, over the Monte Cristo's he first picked out, and with them some matches, and a small pocket-sized bottle of good, seven-year old blended rum.

Fernando and Raul observed from afar. The great statue of Che protectively overlooked the people of the town, the workers in the fields, the students in the schools, and the young boys playing stick ball in the grass down the hill. Beneath the statue, and the long, decorative wall it sat atop, a museum chronicled the guerilla's life, and a mausoleum held his remains, as well as those of his Bolivian comrades, and an eternal flame, helping illuminate their portraits on the wall of the solemn room. They had both been there before—together, in fact, and now stood watching the American, both privately remembering their last, very different, visit to this place.

Instead of snapping photos, or buying a ticket and entering the memorial, Sourdough sought a position in the front, where they sometimes set out chairs to commemorate anniversary calendar dates. He sat down, took out a cigar, used his back and hands to shield the match from the wind, lighting it, getting a strong puff going and taking out the rum. He rotated smokes and steady slugs from the glass bottle, sometimes looking thoughtfully at the statue, sometimes at the traffic, or the handful of tourists moving in pairs or packs, or at the security guard whose primary responsibility was making sure no one took a photo of Che's back, maintaining an unusual level of reverence.

As he smoked, Gabrel thought of the salesman in the cigar shop. They had spoke for a short time about the process of rolling the cigars, the pride the employees took in their finished products, and the symbolism connecting the rolls and the people of the island. Every cigar consisted of three inner leaves of generally poor quality, of no significance beyond their ability to burn. Then there was the flavor leaf, most valuable of all, the life-giver from which the cigar got its name, from which a plantation made its reputation. Finally there was the outer leaf, chosen strictly for its appearance, and worth nothing beyond its attractiveness to the eye, due to the consistency of its color or the strong look of a vein.

The fact of the matter was that many so-called "aficionados" chose based on appearance, based on the outer leaf. But even an expert would not know for sure what they were getting until they lit the tobacco, inhaled the smoke, and tasted the power of the quality hidden from view. It was the story of every cigar. And, according to the shop owner, the story of Cuba.

Hours passed, twilight approached, and Gabrel's posture gradually slumped into a wasted slouch, the bottle nearly empty and the second cigar nearly ashed out. Fernando and Raul kept their watch, now much less concerned with being spotted, and a little more worried what would happen to the operative.

"I'm not sure he will make it back into town, Raul. He's looking awfully rough."

"Maybe I should go finish him off."

"I'm serious. He passes out there he's going to be arrested, you know. That might be inconvenient. He seems oddly melancholy about Guevara, don't you think?"

"Maybe he's a romantic. Communism is irresistible to romantics."

"Well, I'm hungry. Should we go find some food, and hope he doesn't get you in any trouble, hermano?"

Fernando was teasing him now. He knew Raul would not have contacts worth much in Santa Clara, and had guessed correctly that he was under orders not simply to monitor movements from a distance, but to maintain the status quo. The American looked utterly smashed, lurching suddenly to his feet and fighting against the laws of physics, stumbling back toward the lights of the town. There was not a policia presence like Habana, but it was true, any officer would lock him up and report the incident, which would only bring more heat down on Raul.

This man, who had given him his still-throbbing headache, was the only known piece of a puzzle that could be much larger. As long as they had him, they had a hand in play. If Raul allowed him to be neutralized, there was no telling what contingency actions that might trigger. So just as he could not take advantage of this opportunity to return a crushing blow to the side of the head, he also could not allow the American's odd, out of character, out of control drunkenness to be the mistake that took them both out of relevance.

He only made it a few hundred meters, safely out of sight of the monument's security before wilting in a pile of body parts, in the field where the young boys had played stick ball all afternoon. It was as wise a spot as he could've passed out in, where a few hours of sleep would bring him around, and from where he could probably gather himself enough to finish the trek to his room.

But Raul could not take that risk, and watch it work against him from afar. With Fernando smirking all the way, they retrieved his cab, lifted the young American, helped him into it, and rode with him back to the casa particular. It was an unthinkable position for Raul, an opportunity to sift through the little black back pack, to review the information in the notebook, and possibly the photos on the camera. It was like he was taking an exam, and the professor had given him the answer key and walked out of the room with a wink.

The wink was Fernando. His behavior did not make sense; his smugness, his abandoned concerns for his job security, and his original resentment for the new operative. The American sat slouched between them, slobbering a little, mumbling incomprehensible nothings. Fernando had not said a word, and himself had not made any move to search the possessions for answers. Raul thought about killing them both, right then, and dealing with the paperwork and fallout later instead of dealing with the anxiety and questions beating on his brain right now.

They stopped, lifted his body out onto the front stoop, knocking plenty loud enough on the door, and heading off toward the town center.

*   *   *   *

He had called for his military fatigues, and he looked them over now, where they lay on the bed, from his wheelchair, checking to make sure nothing was out of place or missing. His goal for the night, before going to sleep, was not just to see his reflection in the uniform, but to put on every piece on his own. The boots, of course, would be the hardest task. But if he got that far, that would be enough.

With great concentration, he pushed himself up, out of the chair, locking his knees at first, for a step, then relaxing a little. He had a trainer working with him every day, so the legs were as strong—or almost as strong—as if he were walking around all the time. Barbuda checked his posture in the mirror on the wall, and his untrimmed beard; so grey, like what was left of the hair on his head. Objectively, he had to admit he looked very wise, and strong.

The American had overplayed his hand, tipped it, and was now on the run, likely hoping his country would not totally abandon him as punishment for the misstep. That was always the extreme thing about them, how afraid they were of anything outside of the over-detailed plan. They had no understanding of variance, or how to train flexible thinkers. The truth was, this young man probably had more intelligence and guts and ability to succeed than anyone Comandante might pair him against. But his raw talents had been forced through a meat grinder, and he'd come out the other end a robot, sent to out-guerilla a bunch of guerillas. They had again sent a cock to a dogfight.

The spirit was in an unusually ornery mood this evening, only further improving Comandante Barbuda's disposition. "There are too many loose ends here, I wouldn't be so confident if I was standing where you are."

"You're probably right. But I'm more amused than confident."

"Bullocks you are."

"After all this time, they are still so rigidly noncommittal."

"Meaning you admit they could have you if they really put in the effort."

"Meaning I don't even have to raise a defense, they lay their own minefields. Come on, you're as good at sniffing an ending as I am, if not better. He's no decoy. We've been all over every entry, every old player. Most have been out of the loop or disengaged for so long, they'd be useless to re-employ. There are a few variables, but we could neutralize the whole team in a phone call."

"He's still awfully unsubtle."

"Maybe they've wasted so much time waiting for me to lose my edge, they lost theirs."

"I wouldn't make a habit of that kind of thinking."

"Nor I. Now stay if you like, and watch me get into this uniform. I know how much you dislike it. Maybe more than you dislike me."

"No, not more."

Day 9

The ride to Santiago de Cuba felt a lot bumpier than it probably was, felt a lot longer than it probably was, and hurt a lot more than it probably should have, Gabrel finally stepping out of the bus, into another starry sky in a new place, this time with the burden of a dehydrated hangover, and a bit of a stomach virus, to add degrees of difficulty to the task of finding a room for the night. He had vomited at least twice; once in the bathroom of the Santa Clara casa particular, a fact he did not directly recall, but realized the next morning when he tried to sit down on a toilet seat that was spackled with orange chunks of half-digested food. The second occasion he understood in clearer detail, as did all of the passengers on the cruiser, since the bus had to pull to the side of the road for him to finish what he'd started on his lap, in the seat. Rather than dealing with the smell of his t-shirt, he'd taken it off, tossed it into a roadside bush, and rummaged for another in his pack while the driver cleaned out the mess, and the other riders took a cigarette break. If they were amused, or even perturbed, they hid the fact well. More the case, they were conditioned to inconveniences.

It was actually so late in Santiago, nearly three o'clock in the morning, only two taxi drivers waited hopefully at the terminal. The bus line did not make its money from tourists, or from lower class laborers who commuted to work—there was another, less comfortable line specifically for them. The buses Gabrel rode on were relatively new, part of a generous business deal with China, as he understood it, and were mostly the carrier for citizens traveling on business, or to visit family on other parts of the island. There were terminals in or on the edge of every modestly sized town, some much smaller than Santa Clara. These stops, and drop offs, led to the late arrival.

This was not Habana, either, and the two "taxi drivers" anxiously led Sourdough to where their cars were parked outside. They were not yellow cabs, or even the old US models with the lit-up taxi signs. They were just two cars, two regular, piece of shit cars, with no legitimate markings or legal responsibilities. Lazily, Gabrel opted for the paler-skinned of the two drivers, slid into the front seat of his small red sedan, stared at him impatiently as the man failed once, then again, then a third time to get the car started. Finally the other "taxi" agreed to jump start his battery, Sourdough's commitment to the driver painfully past a point of no return. He was tired, and irritated, but soon they were rolling, the car screeching, almost whining as it shifted gears. Gabrel took a deep breath. He had to remember, this was Cuba, and getting angry meant assigning blame, and assigning blame was a Rubix cube. The driver assured him that he knew of a casa particular, and they whizzed around the dead, empty streets without any sightings of life forms, or sounds but the scratchy car radio.

The evening got worse before it got better, the driver pulling to a stop in front of a well-lit house, Gabrel eagerly stepping out with his bag, only to be told that this was not the final destination. While he waited, leaning against the still-running car, a young local man spilled out of the place, onto the front porch, with an even younger local girl and a very drunk Brit. The Brit—blonde, with big teeth, and a bottle of wine in one hand, his opposite arm around the girl's waste, welcomed Sourdough with a lively "Hello, there!" and offered a drink of the booze.

"I'm from 'ove, southern coast, 'ow 'bout you?"

"Edmonton."

"Canada?"

"Yeah."

"I'm ridin' my bicycle aroun' the world, that's 'ow I came to be 'ere, 'ow 'bout you?"

"Nothing quite that exciting."

"You know, you sound more American than Canadian. I already rode through there, you sound a lot like them."

The Brit, named Jason, was wasted. He kept going on and on about this bicycle trip, a pretty original excuse to party with Caribbean girls, which he kept mentioning as the best part of the journey thus far. The girl was attractive enough; black, younger-looking than Sandra, and probably no older than sixteen. But she spoke English well, and was very engaged. Under other circumstances he might have suggested some kind of arrangement, but Gabrel was too tired for it, and too angry his driver had not come back out of the house.

"'ow long you 'ere for?"

The Brit looked amused. Everything about the situation was irritating; them looking down at him from the stoop, he standing there with his bag, looking lost, them floating their discussion in and out of Spanish and English, fully certain he could not comprehend, and ultimately that this great cyclist—who did not even look very fit—was probably less than an hour from sex, whereas Gabrel had no real estimate of when he would finally crawl into bed, knowing only that when it happened, he would be alone.

* * * *

Three days had passed since the Americano left town, plenty of time for Sandra to emotionally readjust, to fall into a new rhythm. He truly surprised her with the abrupt exit; she could see in his face that it was more a device to make the situation easy for him than something designed for her benefit. When she walked away that morning, she had only two things on her mind—telling Lazaro, and dealing with his anger, and then finding a new man, any man, to do whatever it took to forget about the past few days.

But Lazaro had other ideas. He did not bother to explain, but he had a revised strategy. The way he spoke to her—often even harsher directions than before, though just as frequently revealing tenderness entirely new to his character—and the way he managed his time, and hers, led Sandra to wonder what all the commotion was about. Lazaro believed the Americano would return, that he would return for Sandra, and that this made it necessary, since his arrival could be imminent, to keep her as available as reasonably possible.

For the first time, she felt bitter toward his direction. He suggested she go see her abuelita, check how she was doing and stay near to the phone. It was unusually generous of him, but no work also meant no cut. This was more punishment than reward, and Lazaro knew it—she would pass the days at her grandmother's re-thinking her decision to let the Americano leave without paying. Lazaro was always a few steps ahead of her thinking, which was why Sandra suspected he realized how eager she was to move on. The handsome young man with the charming tendencies had hit a nerve; there was an emotional element, a dark stimulus, a weakness deep inside Sandra preventing her from dealing with him in the calculated manner reality required.

Lazaro definitely recognized this, and was not about to let her get off easy, and risk a repeat failure somewhere down the road. Sandra would have to dwell on the situation; with time Lazaro expected her bitterness to shift. The Americano was the one who was ripping her off; he was the one taking advantage of her good faith, and her feminine delusions.

When the traveler returned, Lazaro would call, and he would take her to him, and he would not say a word, not give any new direction or issue any threats. Because time, at her abuelita's, would have permanently corrected Sandra's perspective. She could see in his eyes that he knew this, and she was realizing it was probably the case. He sent her away, with nothing, to think, and to wait, and to gradually despise the Americano, who was wealthy enough to journey the world, and clever enough to enjoy a woman's pleasures at the discount price of a few cheap cans of beer and two tickets to a ball game.

*   *   *   *

Fernando, like many visitors, and many Cubanos, as well, considered Santiago de Cuba the finest city on the island. Its history and culture were much richer, far more interesting than Habana's, and it was only the far-Eastern position, and proximity to the American base in Guantanamo, that kept it from being the undisputed crown jewel of possibly the entire Caribbean. As a boy, his mother had brought him here often, as part of their mysteriously strategic movements, coordinated to accommodate the occasional rendezvous with his father. Because of this, and all of the legendary activities tied to the narrow streets, the city held a certain magic for him.

Last night, Raul had behaved like a nervous old woman about to board an airplane for the first time. He had been holding his tongue thus far on the trip, but Fernando's decision not to follow the American's taxi irritated him greatly. It was evident he did not hold Santiago in the same esteem, and, like Batista's army, was ravaged with insecurity at the great distance between him and his home base in the capitol city. When Fernando explained that he had some contacts, that a few phone calls in a few hours would give him the operative's housing selection, the news only irritated Raul more. It was as if he forgot how long they had been maneuvering against one another, and how parallel their support networks sometimes turned out to be.

He could see the fiery distrust in Raul. Every time Fernando smiled, or made a joke, or made light of the situation, or brushed off a concern without care, he could sense the swelling animosity. Neither man knew if he was the better informed; Fernando, truthfully, was going entirely on gut instinct; on a hunch and a hope the situation would ultimately clarify itself with enough time and flexibility to react to it. He had no explanation for the incident at the ball park, but he was equally determined not to fall into the extreme paranoia that had overwhelmed Raul; a signal his old friend, and the people he represented, were feeling unusually exposed and vulnerable. Whether the operative was a legitimate threat was one consideration; a new consideration, for Fernando, was the possibility that Raul's aggressive pursuit might reveal the kind of opportunity to dramatically alter the status quo that aggressive moves on Fernando's part could never achieve. He talked Raul into sharing a hotel room just off of the main square, then made the calls and delivered the information he had promised. The Americano had settled in with a well-known couple only a few blocks away, toward the port. In the morning bustle they could find a decent vantage point and track him from there.

Raul lay down and closed his eyes without another word. Fernando had done all the driving, suspected he would fall asleep first, that Raul might use the opportunity to slip out into the night, and that was fine. As long as he projected confidence, the paranoia would persist, and he would maintain the upper hand. Even without the usual before-bed rum, Fernando slept considerably well.

Raul did not. As it happened, the unsettling thoughts that kept him awake were built on the same elements which lightly infiltrated Fernando's dreams that night. The thoughts, basically, concerned the very remote possibility of the two of them, and the operative, potentially initiating change that would affect the island's population, without knowing, when they did it, whether that change would be beneficial, or catastrophic.

*   *   *   *

Young Samuel arrived later than usual. On his way home from work he had stopped at a friend's place, and stayed for a late dinner. Now he entered the rooftop apartment to find his grandfather still awake, watching television, and waiting for him. Lazaro had left an hour ago, after a long, heartfelt talk between two friends; filled with warnings, accusations, and sincere goodbyes.

The old man had sorrow in his eyes, and spoke apologetically. "We are leaving tomorrow." It was something they discussed before, but not in a few years, not since Young Samuel started work at the hospital. He sat down on the couch by his grandfather.

"How?"

"Through Mexico. It is the best way, now. No trouble, not so expensive. A guide will take us, to a border crossing at Texas. They have no choice but to let us in from there, and then we can ride a bus to Florida."

"With my English, we should be okay."

"Yes, I think with your English, no problems."

Young Samuel stood, patting his grandfather's leg, moving toward his room. Aside from some clean clothes, the most important thing to pack would be his education documentation. It was possible these were acceptable. And with his English, and the help of his uncles and mother, maybe it would not take too long to find some good work around Miami.

Day 10

Gabrel set out early, once again unable to properly sleep a first night in a new place. The bus ride gave him time to game plan, study the map, city layout, and read brief descriptions of the popular sights, noteworthy tips, and happening nightspots. Even though he could not sleep, just lying in the bed, no movement or burden, proved a solid remedy for the Santa Clara sickness. As he stepped out into the morning, he could feel new strength in his steps.

The narrow streets, steep hills, and dense concentration of houses and buildings made Santiago feel huge. It was very difficult to gain a sense of location, as the sprawl of city blocks spilled indefinitely in every direction. For a while Gabrel just walked, falling into the flow of pedestrians and expecting to eventually come across a park or church or museum or hotel that would register with the memory of what he'd read, and randomly serve as an anchor point for the day's explorations.

As he walked, his eye began to highlight the attractive females occasionally passing by. Old Samuel had told him he would like Santiago, had mentioned something in his mumbling, accented Spanish about the beauty of the women there, and Gabrel let the comment drop, since Sandra had been in the room. But now that he was on site, thoughts of more interaction, of a two or three day experience to contrast with Sandra, and Habana, seemed like a valid use of evening hours. Again, there were many policia, but surely, he expected, the Lazaro's of this population would spot him before he identified them, and he would once again do best by cautiously following their seasoned processes.

Gabrel settled into a seat in a balcony restaurant; part of a well-known hotel from the old era, overlooking a well-groomed park bordered on the other three sides by a church, a bank, and a government building. It was as close a replication of Habana Viejo as Santiago was willing to offer. In the morning air, the tourists and policia seemed just as formal, just as legitimate, as those in the other city. But something in their posture hinted at reduced formality here, and something Old Samuel had mentioned resonated with Sourdough; one of the reasons people came to Santiago was to get away from Habana. To a degree, he too had fled, though he did not know exactly what differences to expect, or how to go about submerging in their benefits.

He ordered a mojito, and noticed a very old woman, resting on a bench in the open square, watching her while he waited for his drink. She wore a red dress, old and tattered, but still looking like new in the bright sunlight. Her hair was a very dirty grey, pulled into a loose bun on the back of her head. The woman's skin resembled a tough leather, much like the old man's in Santa Clara. Her lips wrapped around a very large cigar, the kind of such impractical size, to smoke one might take half a day, and for a tourist, or youth unaccustomed to the strength, the effort might leave you hospitalized. But hers was lit, and she was smoking, and the way she reclined on the bench told Gabrel she would be there longer than he would bother to watch. The way she kept her gaze, as so many on this island could, steady, looking at nothing in particular, told him the doses of smoke only tickled her lungs. She looked at least eighty, and, like the man in Santa Clara, had developed her own consistent purpose. Just as he repeatedly re-lived fantasies, this woman in Santiago humbled the great product of her land—the formidable tobacco. She was a testament to the power these people exuded, each in their own unique way. It was alarming, their inner strength.

The balcony was busy this morning, mostly with guests of the hotel, who paid the inflated drink prices in exchange for the god-like view over the square, and for the safety of their numbers. It was the reason he would only have one drink, his mojito a private toast to the building, which had been included in a literary work he was fond of; a portrait of bygone glory days.

Gabrel had begun to recognize a layer of self-disgust in his tendency to disassociate from the others who were not so different as he wanted to believe. He was just as incapable of blending into the local fray, he was just as apprehensive to trust, he was just as willing to take advantage of the moral desperation brought about by their economic shortfalls. It had become too apparent to ignore, his hypocrisy. Perhaps what bothered him most was that, inevitably, he would be as comfortable with being separate, with being an intrusion, as the rest of the pale-skinned jet-setters, instead of succeeding in the opposite direction, and achieving some sort of cohabitation between the two worlds; something to make him feel less repulsive.

Gabrel quickly sipped down the rum cocktail. He needed to walk off his frustration and find something in this city to satisfy his coming here; to justify the long bus ride. Sooner or later, he had to return to Habana, and face down the demons of that place. But he knew he wasn't ready for that showdown yet; what he needed was new motivation.

* * * *

Fernando and Raul kept a distant pace with Gabrel the whole day. They followed him to the Moncada Barracks, where he slowly roamed the grounds, studied the bullet marks still visible in the bright yellow walls, and peaked in on the students inside, deep in their studies and cute in their dark purple uniforms.

"He seems to know the significance," commented Fernando.

"Their version, at least," Raul replied, unimpressed.

They followed him through the streets, to a small house, as ordinary as every one around it, where he dipped inside, paying surprising respect to the Pais brothers.

"Do you think he admires their courage?" Fernando asked.

"Or celebrates their assassinations."

The American lingered in the house for a solid hour before moving on, through the heart of the city, across to the far end, where the grand cemetery held the bodies of many of the national heroes. They watched from afar as he wandered among the graves, sitting for a while on a bench near some stones marked with the "26 July" black and red flags, highlighting their contributions, then again at the extravagant tomb of Jose Marti, watching the hourly changing of the guard and scribbling in his notebook.

This display of disrespect for the father of the country was more than Raul could bear. He had never had an opinion on tourists before. Now, seeing strangers, and enemies, permitted to desecrate such holy ground with their self-serving presence, it did not seem right, not at all. He did not blame the American, but turned his anger toward the cemetery employees, who so graciously admitted him with smiles, and the Honor Guard that stood at attention, their uniforms so sharp, their medals so unwarranted as they permitted the operative to lean lazily on the walls, to sit on the steps of the memorial. The more he watched, the more his anger fermented. He blamed the policia on the street, for letting such an imposter move about unimpeded, free to encourage the corruption of the desperate youth. He blamed the taxi drivers, who gladly chauffeured him around town, eagerly made friendly conversation, all in exchange for a few modest bills. He blamed the bus drivers, and ticket sellers at the terminals. He blamed the passengers who sat next to him, accepting his presence. He blamed the airport customs and immigration personnel for letting him pass.

Mostly, of course, Raul blamed himself. The stress of the past few days, time spent reflecting on his poor judgment at the baseball game, had developed in him a sense of patriotic guilt that he had never felt before. He was in a unique position to squash this threat, though he had been ordered only to observe and report; essentially, to tolerate such offensive behavior, so long as it was not overtly aggressive.

What would his superiors think of this, if they were watching with him? Could they restrain their own rage, as they expected his to be restrained? Would they categorize this as tolerable, would they deny it an act of aggression? Did they think him unpatriotic, or did they not consider this spot as hallowed as he—and so many Cubanos—did?

Fernando could not deny his own emotions, watching as the American finally left the steps of the memorial, his notebook again tucked securely into the small back pack. He walked slower now, not just from fatigue or sore feet. His head slightly tilted forward, he was no longer interested in the sights and sounds of the city. He looked burdened, more than anything. They followed him all the way back to the park. Instead of shuffling into the hotel, for another round on the balcony, the American slid into a nameless bar off of a side street, away from the traffic and the eyes of turistas and policia.

Fernando turned to Raul, and could see that his tension had not subsided in the least. "Looks like he's going to tie another one on."

"You can count me out, no lifeguard this time. I don't care who this bastard thinks he is, or who anybody else thinks he is. He gets arrested, its his own fault, and its your boss's fault for trusting the task to a drunkard."

"I think we should go talk to him. Let's give him an hour, if he's still inside, let's go for a drink."

Raul eyed him suspiciously. Absorbed in guilt as he'd been for the last few hours, he'd forgotten that more than anyone else, even more than the American, and the American's managers, he resented Fernando. If there was one more thing to feel guilty about, it was the years he'd misused befriending the only traitor to the fatherland he'd ever met.

"This is all in the script for you, isn't it?"

"Don't be ridiculous," Fernando replied. He concentrated his stare, knowing Raul would read too much into a blink, or any hesitation toward eye contact. "I'll be straight with you. I think we're chasing our tails. I think this guy is having second thoughts. I don't know why he's here, I don't know what he's having second thoughts about, but I'm willing to risk letting you in on that secret if it means finding it out myself. And if he's part of something big, we better take a shot at getting involved before he comes around to his senses and we lose the high ground."

Raul looked away, at the door to the bar the American had walked through. "Speak for yourself," he said, but made no attempt to leave, and suggested no ulterior course of action. For all he knew, the operative was waiting inside the door, stone-sober, for Fernando to lead Raul to the trap. On most days, he would have found a way to wiggle out of it, but his juices were flowing; he was primed for an altercation. It was time enough to make a play at Fernando, too. If he was part of the operation, better to find out for sure now—and get rid of him—than have to continue to juggle the two threats. After all, Higher wanted the American observed, but untouched. They put no such restrictions on Fernando.

Raul followed his old friend inside. The lighting was not very good, the kind of place people went because they felt more comfortable in the shadows. Only a handful of patrons were there, two on stools at the bar, another pair at a far table, near the restroom, the bartender in a soft conversation with the security guard, and the American, who sat facing the door, his notebook open, a mojito half-gone, and his eyes on them expectantly. Really he was watching Fernando, who casually approached and sat down, without asking permission. Raul followed suit, noticing that the American did not realize the pair were together until they were both sitting across from him.

So close, face to face now, even in the shadows Raul could see the operative had young eyes, but he was not as youthful or green as he looked from afar. The pace of his breathing had quickened, and he'd closed the notebook, his hand resting palm-down on top of it, protectively. Raul expected the other hand to disappear beneath the table, perhaps to a weapon in a pocket. Instead, it reached for the drink, lifting the glass to his mouth. Fernando maintained a polite smile, and Raul realized the two of them did not know each other, or at least were going to play out such roles. He had always been the superior chess player, but now felt too short on patience, the others willing to let the silence rule.

"If I really gave a damn what was in there," Raul started, nodding with his head toward the notebook, "I would have read through it in Santa Clara."

The American looked him over, the way a customer inspects merchandise, with a careful eye for blemishes. It lasted only a minute, but Raul bristled, and hated himself for letting it bother him. The operative looked back at Fernando, then down at his drink as he spoke.

"The history of this place is incredible. You can feel it. I don't mean at the monuments, or in the museums. I mean in the streets between them, and in these little bars and restaurants along these alleys. I get the idea this place has always been a bar, for hundreds of years, and these are the same avenues horses and wagons used to roll on. Marti might have sat in this bar. Who knows what it was called then, who was serving the drinks, but he might have sat here, got drunk, and stumbled home on a regular basis."

"Is that why you're here?" Fernando joined into the conversation. "You know, you're talking about a great man. Don't you think we might take exception to you calling him a drunk?" Fernando leaned forward, a posture meant to intimidate, or at least send a signal of seriousness. The words and the move took Raul by surprise, as did the way Fernando continued, before the American could muster a response.

"You seem to have a weakness for our rum. You seem to rely on it to help you deal with your thoughts. Well, I've done that a lot, myself. But mostly when I've either been upset at a decision I made, something stupid I did, or when I had a decision to make, and I already had a pretty good idea I was going to mess it up solid."

The American finished his drink, turned to the bartender and gestured for him to make three more, turning back to Fernando and Raul with a grin. "You know, never heard of the Pais brothers before I got here. You need a Marti, sure, but you need fellas like that just as much. The kind willing to do the dirty, unsung jobs, take the heat off of the big guns. I betcha they both knew they'd never see a victory parade, just as sure as they were that victory was possible. You don't find that kind of selfless service, that kind of real fearlessness, in a lot of people. Can't be taught or trained, I think."

The drinks arrived, and the American raised his in a toast. "I'm hoping to make it up to San Juan Hill before I catch a bus to Bayamo."

Raul wanted to make a comment about the century-old battle, but Fernando leaned forward, speaking first. "I suppose we'll head toward Bayamo, too. You don't want to save on the bus fare?"

"Naw, I don't mind the bus. The seats don't recline so well, but I like getting sleep in transport, so I can arrive with enough energy to explore a little bit." The American took a sip of his mojito, setting the glass down on the table. He grinned again, and looked so deceptively young, Raul wanted to wrap his hands around the throat, and choke him, strangle him, just to see the eyes bulge, the mouth gasp for air, just to see something genuine and definitely authentic.

There was not much more conversation, Raul eventually joining Fernando and finishing off his drink. The American left the bar first, announcing sore feet from the day's walking and blaming his sandals, which needed replaced. Then he was gone, and they let him go, and had another drink each, and Raul felt very confused and uncomfortable about the situation, and what his superiors might think of it, and how disadvantaged his position had become.

* * * *

With a lightning-fast right hook, Lazaro sent Sandra reeling, the back of her head smacking into the corner of the room, her knees buckling as she fell to the ground, lifting her arms in front of her face to shield herself from another blow. He did not honor her retreat, lunging toward her, lifting her from the ground by her elbows, his anger doubling his strength as he tossed her toward the bed, and her momentum threw her over it, tumbling into a bruised ball on the floor on the other side. By now the man was gone, fled into the afternoon traffic, leaving her, naked and sobbing, to absorb the brunt of Lazaro's rage. He moved toward her again, and she wrapped her arms tightly around his knees, ducking her head against his skinny legs. He pulled her up by her hair, seating himself on the edge of the bed, bending her over his knee, and slapping her buttocks with hard, stiff blows until she stopped sobbing, stopped making any sound at all, and he let her slide off of his leg, into a mess again on the floor.

She knew she dared him to do it, disregarding his generous offer of a few days break, to spend with her abuelita and wait for the Americano. Instead, she'd grown bored, impatient, resentful of Lazaro's high esteem of the turista and at the same time unable to keep herself from fondly lusting for him. The long hours of lonely nights reinforced the passionate memories, dimmed her recollection of the frustration of pacing Old Samuel's apartment, fearing he'd return with her replacement. There was also the matter of her being broke, and with Lazaro having no intention of helping, she'd gone to a reliable source, and tried to erase all her problems on the sneak.

It was the principle of the betrayal that bothered him most. Sandra could not survive a week without him, he knew it, she was far too irrational in her decisions, emotion-driven, and incapable of predicting cause and effect. She was bleeding a little from the lip, and her left cheek was already turning a purple hue.

The Americano would not respond well to this, but the odds were he would not return for a few days, and better that Lazaro was certain she would spend those in-doors, healing and nursing wounds, than have to worry she might be moving behind his back and jeopardizing the situation.

    He lifted her up by her elbows again, flinging her onto the bed. Sandra looked up at him, her chin trembling only a little. The first day he'd found her, he told her how magnificent her eyes were. Wide and unblinking now, they were neither afraid nor apologetic, but still held a certain faithfulness he recognized. She was a pretty good kid, and might not have a very big brain, but she would not leave him, or hurt him intentionally. All the action had fired him up, and seeing that she would die at his hand before she gave her loyalty to another, the evidence of his power pumped strongly through his body. Lazaro took hold of her legs, below the knee, using them to turn Sandra gently onto her belly, repositioning them, unzipping his trousers, and pulling her toward him.

Day 11

Bayamo reminded Gabrel a lot of Santa Clara, but any images of Che were replaced, here, with statues and murals of Cespedes, the bearded revolutionary whose legacy preceded Marti's. They were all chapters of the same book now, cleverly tied together as approving forefathers of the modern, ever-ongoing movement. He'd arrived in the early afternoon, hiked from the terminal to the town's dominant square, and plopped down on a bench, his pack resting next to him, to linger a while and get a gauge on the people and possibilities before searching out a bed.

Within minutes, a dark-skinned young man in decent clothes, wearing a ball cap that displayed an homage to the September 11th, 2001 terrorist attacks, sat down on the bench beside him, offering chewing gum, and then cigarettes, and asking a lot of questions, hoping for a way to accommodate in exchange for the lightest degree of friendship. He was younger than Gabrel by a few years, his name was Thomas, and despite being confined to the modest-sized town, his English was even better than Lazaro's.

"You are from America? Where in America?"

"Los Angeles."

"Ah, Los Angeles! Man, that is great. It is an honor to meet someone from Los Angeles, I feel honor to meet you. Why you come to Bayamo?"

"Comandancia de la Plata."

"Ah, yes! Of course! Wonderful! You come all the way from Los Angeles to see this, you will love it, I have been there, you will love it! You will go in the morning?"

"Yes."

"Yes! Of course you will! It is an honor for me to meet someone from Los Angeles. Wow. I love America! I love this place you are from!"

If a young Cuban man approached him on a similar public bench in Habana, they would not last very long before the policia approached and scared them away. Thomas harbored no such fears, his smile seemed sincere, and his eagerness to speak English and show off his hat was incredible to Gabrel, considering the remoteness of their location. This was possibly the only hustler in town, just as he was possibly the only prospect to be hustled. The combination, and the boy's energy, diffused any hostility. He seemed harmless, and there was a full night to burn before the early morning jaunt out into the countryside, to the national park, and the hike to his next destination.

"You like baseball? There is a game here tonight. The Industrials are here tonight, everybody will go!"

The opportunity to catch the "real" Habana team was too good to pass up. Thomas agreed to meet at the same spot in a few hours, giving Gabrel the break to find a casa particular near by, take a nap and gather his thoughts. It was evident Thomas had no further plans, and would likely stay in the park waiting until the designated hour, or go to his home and sit there staring at the clock. But Gabrel did not want to encourage another Lazaro-type situation; he had lied, in fact, claiming to already have room reservations and need no assistance, just to avoid being indebted or, worse, fully exposed.

* * * *

Thomas returned with a friend that evening, a smiling Cubano who lacked English, and who carried himself in more of a street-wise way. The walk to the baseball stadium took them a half hour, Thomas dominating the conversation with descriptions of his job—as a chess instructor at the local academy—and of the town's weekend evening tradition of setting up tables in the park, and citizens of all ages participating, matching wits and styles. He joked that this was the wrong place for a part-time player to take on even the youngest of school children, and Gabrel believed him. They stopped at a small shop along the way, Sourdough happily agreed to Thomas' suggestion of buying three cans of beer and a pack of cigarettes, and the trio drank them and smoked as they continued on, further and further from the quaint town center.

The stadium indeed was packed to near capacity, Gabrel paying for the tickets, another round of beers, and the group finding space to sit down the first base line. Everything about the Industrials team gave the impression of superiority; their uniforms were made of better fabric, their cleats were of a foreign, imported brand, and their shoulders and forearms were larger, their body language more confident, and their gaze distant and bored, like a venerable champion. Many of the fans wore New York Yankee hats, shirts, and jackets; a reference to recent defectors who had proven Cuba's talent with their dominance on the great American stage. Even tonight, there were possibly scouts in the stands, checking pitch velocity with hidden radar guns, or timing a center fielder's sprint out of the batter's box on a stopwatch.

Thomas understood the connection between his nation's pastime and the Great Enemy, who introduced them to it, taught them the tricks and continued to offer millions of dollars and dream opportunities to their stars. In a sea of islands where natives measured their worth by the world's sport, soccer, Cuban children dreamed of heroics on the diamond, and Cuban professional players dreamed secretly of Yankee Stadium on chilly October nights.

It was impossible for Gabrel to follow the game as he wanted, relaxed, responding to the vibes of the crowd and harmlessly cheering along. Thomas' appetite for all things American spurred him to ask nonstop questions, about everything from the variety of cars to the variety of people to the variety of fast food restaurants. Gabrel could see his pride, his swelling chest, as he recited the facts that he knew, about places like Washington D.C., and about obscure national semi-celebrities, from Monica Lewinsky to O.J. Simpson. To listen and nod attentively meant encouraging, and practically asking for more of the same, but Gabrel played the part. Thomas had mentioned a club they could go to after the game, in a confident way that agreed with Sourdough's evening aspirations.

By the seventh inning the allure was gone. Bayamo's home team gave it their all, but was overmatched by the talent of the great behemoths. Thomas suggested they go, reading Gabrel's expression and checking his watch, sure the club would be open by now. Unlike in the US, the rest of the crowd was not going anywhere. Traffic would not be an issue, since almost everyone walked to the game. And alternatives for entertainment were limited, not to mention a consensus desire to get the most out of the money spent on tickets. This was not the option they most preferred, the way some, in other places, live by the buffet; this was the option they'd been given, and better to enjoy it than spend the time in darker thoughts.

The threesome trekked a few blocks to the promised dance club, finding it closed, much to Thomas' surprise, and much less to the surprise of his shifty-eyed friend. Fortunately there was a back-up plan, and as the distant sound of a jubilant crowd signaled a dramatic home team comeback, Gabrel and his guides walked even further away from his casa particular, to the kind of high class hotel where he would never think to get a room, and where Thomas assured him there was a quality bar, and that this was a standard rendezvous point for his fun-loving friends.

The evening deteriorated at a disappointingly rapid swing. Thomas did have a collection of amigos there, but it was Gabrel he turned to for the first bottle of rum, originally meant to be split between the three of them, balanced and flavored by a can of Sprite. When the group gathered round it was emptied quite fast, and it was Gabrel he turned to for a second bottle, and some more cans of Sprite, mostly to satisfy the girls, with their highly-selective taste buds. Gabrel had mentioned, a few times, his need to wake early, in order to coordinate transportation, complete the hike, and make it back for a bus out of town in a busy blur of tomorrow. Now he was realizing, slightly slower than the rhythm of Thomas' suggestions, that his newest "friend" did not see a conflict between his current methods of spending every dollar Gabrel had, and Sourdough's overall goals for this phase of the trip. It was disappointing, that he would have to end things dramatically, and outside of the spirit of Life Immediate. But Thomas practically dared him to protest the faux-hospitality.

The effort would have been worth nothing in Habana. There were girls, but they seemed attached to the opportunistic guys present, all of them in on the scam. Gabrel paid for everything, from those first cans of beers at the small store on the street to now, suggestions of a need for a third bottle, or, an alternative presented, the entire party moving to the hotel's dance club, which was dead for the mid-week evening, but still offered bumping sounds that would get the girls gyrating, not to mention offering even more outlandishly overpriced drinks.

It was the next exchange, when Gabrel mentioned that he wanted to leave, and a now-drunk Thomas pretended not to understand, laughing as he asked it be repeated, that the evening hit its climactic low-point. Sourdough excused himself to the restroom, wandering out of the hotel, into the parking lot and quiet, small town night. Once outside, he realized that he was drunk, too. Worse, he realized the hour was late, taxis did not circulate around here, and he would have to walk all the way back to the town's center, guessing the direction, feeling disoriented.

His first stab only tired his legs, wasting a half-hour and bringing him round in a circle back to the hotel. By that point Thomas and the others, drunk and without money, had spilled onto the street. The confrontation was awkward, annoying. Gabrel was outnumbered, out of his element, and considered the conflicting possibilities of smashing Thomas' nose and being beaten and robbed by the mob of them. He yielded to self-preservation, moving out, ignoring their calls for reconciliation, in a direction opposite theirs, even though they obviously knew the right course, and this meant taking the long way to nowhere.

More than dehydrated, or tired, or angry, Gabrel felt disgusted by the night's happenings. For all his distrust of Lazaro, he had at least silently respected the man as a learned tradesman. It was more of a challenge, matching wits with the old, wiry jinitero. Thomas was just a kid who grew up feeling slighted by his predicament, who had figured out a way to turn his self-pity and bitterness toward the Super Power into a mock-admiration hustle scheme. He had no experience but that of a small town hick. He teased Gabrel with offers of nothing more spectacular than one-night friendship. Yet the low-grade chess teacher, whose game seemed so much more like checkers, had milked the situation. And now, while Sourdough walked, unsure of the distance, having to deal with the taste of disgust in his mouth, he knew Thomas, probably only a few blocks away, was wearing a Kasparov grin.

Day 12

The ride to the foot of the mountain, the National Park entrance, was expensive. The only alternative heading there out of Bayamo was a commissioned taxi, and one-way at that. This was deep Cuba now, as rural and third world as the island could get. These farmers along the roadside, driving cattle, sleeping under thatched-roofing, were peasants, just as their great-grandparents had been. It was a fact beyond denial, their time-warp existence as un-ignorable as the roadside murals, commemorating members of the Granma landing who never made it to the first rally point.

Maneuvering from the park entrance to the foot of the trail, regrettably, required another shuttle, all but destroying any feel of authenticity. On top of this was the requirement to have a guide, for Gabrel a tall, slender man who looked capable of marathons, to ensure respectful, hands-off observation and further trounce any hope of thoughts melting into fantasies of running the trail with the guerillas, in the rugged glory days before responsibility sobered their storytelling. By the time they finally got going, Gabrel had forgot about the bottle of rum he'd packed in his backpack, and had lowered his standards to being thankful they did not have to live down to the snail-like stroll of a group tour. The fact of the matter was, this hike would not be easy. Most tourists budgeted a full day for it, with a night before and after spent in the accommodating hotel at the base of the mountain. Sourdough was budgeting a morning, and his guide proved up to the task. They started out at a hike, only to test the earth. Once Gabrel was confident the ground would hold his step, the route became an obstacle course, hurdling roots and rock obstructions in a race ever upward.

Sourdough had grown up on a mountainside like this, in the formidable Appalachian chain. As a boy, daydreaming of running with Robin Hood passed his hours of play. Now, not just a grown man, but one beyond the trivial expectations of tourism, he let himself feel the spirit of the legends of the hillside. It was easy to slip into childlike imaginations, to visualize others around him, their feet blistered by the only boots available, the skin of their backs broken into rashes from sweat and bug bites. They hurried through the undergrowth, urging him along, rushing back to the encampment safely concealed by the mountain's overgrowth, strategically emplaced to allow retreat at a moment's notice.

By the time they reached the tree houses, still standing as they did a half-century ago, still so modest and un-expectant of glory, still so primitive and basic, Gabrel's chest heaved with the satisfaction of a runner at the end of the effort. The guide, too, needed a moment to catch his breath, before lifting the wall of the main hut, stabilizing it with a pole and pointing out the famous bed, and desk, and refrigerator with the bullet hole in it, just like in the photographs. Gabrel remembered the rum, pulled it out to the delight of his new, tall friend-of-the-moment, and they did not budge from the balcony overlooking the draw until they'd emptied half the contents. It would be a good walk back; an opportunity for the kind of uninterrupted reflection you can't even steal in the city.

They shared a beer at the bar attached to the hotel at the bottom of the mountain. By the mid-afternoon looks of the place, there were not many occupants. Still, the staff did not move about with any fear of pink slips; there would always be anniversary commemorations, which meant there would always be VIP visits, and so always a need for a fine, well-equipped, photogenic establishment.

A thin slice of placid river ran behind the lodging. After a hearty thanks and handshake to his guide, and a politely refused offer to go, and dine, and stay in his humble, thatched home for the evening, Gabrel moved over to the bank of the water, to smoke a cigar and wait for a taxi—summoned by the front desk receptionist—to transport him back to Bayamo.

Standing among the ghosts of the glory days, under the thick, protective blanket of the trees, had revitalized Sourdough. The thought process was admittedly counter-intuitive, not only that he would venture to such a place in search of inspiration, but that he would find it there, along the broken, rocky trail. More moving than the modest headquarters shacks with their primitive living conditions, for Gabrel, was his interaction with the guide. Here was a man who made the most of each day, who clearly loved what he was doing, who could not hide his thrilled approval when the American pulled out a bottle of high quality rum, and offered to share it. He showed no signs of ill will, invested no energy in petitioning for a tip, did not expect Gabrel to pay for his beer, and seemed to offer dinner and a night's bed out of a desire to demonstrate generosity, not as investment with an expected more-than-adequate reimbursement. The innocent smile and healthy stride up the hillside did wonders to wipe the bitterness of the night with Thomas from Gabrel's mouth. It complimented the hideout perfectly; it made sense to begin the Revolution here, among good people with good intentions, worth risking your neck for.

The cigar was part of a four-pack Gabrel bought in Santa Clara. He'd smoked the first two over thoughts of Guevara, and the third during his meditation on Marti. It was impossible to discredit their sincerity, yet nearly as difficult to accurately imagine what they would do now, what they might recommend to him, what options they would reproach, and what measures they'd willingly go to. He had come here, as he had gone there, out of a moral obligation, to himself, to act without ignorance, as well as above the influence of political propaganda.

This cigar held a better taste than the other three had; richer, with an even burn, a great compliment to the day's exercise. The guide, and the hike, brought him back to agreement with his purpose. Gabrel would go back to Habana. He had some time before his departure flight, and now more than ever understood how to make the most of it.

*   *   *   *

The fatigues left a little too much space around the neckline; he'd lost more weight, more muscle weight, than he originally thought. But they still looked good—he still cut the kind of figure eyes wouldn't pass over without a second glance. Comandante Barbuda turned sideways, inspecting his figure, the shine on the leather boots, the clean fold in the pants. He had not put these on in over half a year, and felt thrilled not just to be wearing them, but to be standing in them; the only acceptable position.

The doctors reacted with shock to the rapid improvement; they had served him for years, and still they treated him like a normal patient. Even in Cuba, the medical school professors and senior physicians and surgeons believed accurate medication prescriptions and formula monitoring were the keystones to patient recovery. The fact of the matter, much to the schoolhouse's chagrin, was that ninety percent of rehabilitation was psychological, and those who had a need to recover, or a reason to return to good health, did so at a significantly faster rate than the depressed and down-trodden. Admitting this might reduce their level of importance, but in Barbuda's case, at least, it would reflect better on their common sense.

He used the wheelchair in the morning, sliding into it from his bed, but that was mostly due to habit, not necessity. He stood up from it, walking to shower, his first shower, instead of a sponge bath, in a long time, and the wheelchair still rested where he'd left it that morning, unused and in the way. Tomorrow he would have it carried out and disposed of. For now he had other tasks on his mind, more important efforts. Barbuda moved to his desk, his knees energetically absorbing and powering his steps, challenging him for more of a workout.

There was no question the international press would turn the public appearance into front page, lead-story news, if it only lasted a few minutes, and consisted of nothing more spectacular than a wave of his hand. To show they still meant little more than a distraction to him, to show this was not a performance, but an event with a purpose, his speech would stray from repetitive rhetoric, focus on current events, and fire challenges at the opposition's ears. Because of how they counted him out, because of the weakness of the most recent effort against him, the occasion demanded a memorable display. He would remind them of his resolve, demonstrate how significant he still was, and, most importantly, whip the crowd into a rabid frenzy, just like he used to, just like they needed.

He could still see, from the corner of his eye, his reflection in the mirror on the other side of the room, his back straight in the chair, pen in hand. Barbuda could not help but smile at the thought of including, in the speech, a short mention of how foolish they would feel, if only they knew how poorly he'd been doing, before they brought him back to life.

* * * *

The night sky, the darkness, snuck up on them, as Fernando and Raul both leaned forward, over the chess board drawn onto the top of the table, recharging their plastic cups with the bottle of budget rum that sat between them, most of the pieces still un-blurred. This was the third game, Raul victorious in the first two and already holding Fernando's queen, a knight, and both bishops. They were sitting at an outdoor set-up attached to a small restaurant, across the street from the bus terminal. So far, no sign of the American, but still a few hours until the last run toward Habana before morning.

Raul watched as Fernando contemplated an escape move. They had known each other a long time, never having to overcome the kind of professional conflict experienced the past week. For most of it Raul had been on his heels, but now, passing time with their favorite mutual contest, his performance, as it always did, reinforced his confidence. Fernando was a nice guy who spent most of his life reacting to situations and propositions presented to him. Raul had achieved his position through activism and fearless, persistent volunteering. Sympathy pushed him to pity his adversary, giving him more than the benefit of the doubt on most occasions. Also, this was a lonely job, and there was not exactly a plethora of others who could appreciate the strain.

But that did not excuse the inexcusable treason. At the end of the day, Fernando was working for an organization whose main objective was eliminating Raul and his managers, unseating them from authority and reversing the effect of their efforts. They were at an impasse. As his old friend reached for a rook, another move to stall the inevitable, Raul reached for the piece, grabbing it first, and lifting it from the table to capture Fernando's attention.

"Do you realize, will you at least admit, we are worshipping different religions?"

Fernando nodded, his expression revealing that he knew this conversation was coming. He was a lot better at guessing real world maneuvers than those on the board. "I suppose respectful ignorance is hypocritical."

"It is, Fernando. It is! You and I cannot coexist any longer. I cannot responsibly tolerate your threatening posture. How can you tolerate me?"

"I can't. I like you, but I can't."

"At least I am a patriot, that must make things easier. But you're a traitor, and I cannot ignore it."

"I'm as much for my country as you are. We assign ourselves to opposing politics, but-"

"There are no politics! This is Cuba! You are Cubano! You cannot plead politics or redirect the blame!"

"I'm surprised to hear it from you."

"I hate that I've held it in so long, I make no other apologies!"

"You know, Raul, there was a nation before all this."

"There were Imperialists before all this."

"Yes, there were." Fernando's stare was steady, as was his tone. It kept Raul from interrupting. "But there was a nation, under all of that. There was always a nation, waiting for its chance. Its just that you think its been living and breathing, and I think its still there, held down under a heavy blanket. Only now, we can't blame imperialists."

"You work for them!"

"No. I work for Cuba. For the nation still waiting to happen."
Before they could rise to blows, a dented, rusting blue taxi pulled up to the terminal. Gabrel climbed out, tossing his large back pack over a shoulder and proceeding inside.

* * * *

Lazaro was deep into a disagreement about strategy when the phone call vibrated his mobile, in his pocket. Gustav was a good friend, had been a fighter himself a long time ago, but more of a sparring partner than a legitimate challenger in the ring. He had four children, all boys, all with good, stable jobs, and he himself still working, and yet, when it came to Lazaro, the most he could do was nod in agreement and give way to the stronger position. Especially, but not only, when it came to boxing, as the morning's discussion had, with Gustav ignorantly suggesting advantages to defensive techniques, and Lazaro setting him straight.

"Boxing is not a power match, it's a mind game," Lazaro began, rising as he spoke and taking a solid pugilist stance. "Forget about Savon, and before him, Kid Chocolate, forget what you think you learned from them. The lesson of Savon is not the value of a good defense, it's the dominance of a disguised offense! That's right! There's a difference! If you think he was reacting, you are saying he had no thoughts on his own, only thoughts provided him by his opponent. That's ridiculous! You cannot win through defense! You cannot enter into a battle of any importance with nothing but the hope of your enemy's mismanagement! This is why you sparred, Gustav, this is why you provided me exercise, then watched while I became champion. It has nothing to do with ability, everything to do with approach. I have the talent of an old woman, but the attitude of a tiger. That's why, even now, you wouldn't last two rounds at the end of my jab."

Lazaro reached into his pocket, lifting the old mobile to his ear and smiling unabashedly as Gabrel's voice broke through from the other end.

"Lazaro? This is Gabrel. Lazaro?"
"Yes, yes, man, how are you?"
"I'm in Habana. Can you meet me?"
"Yes, yes, of course, man. Where are you?"
"I'll be at the Hotel Lincoln. Can you make it?"
"Of course, man."
"Can you make it?"

"Yes, yes, of course."
"Alright, I'll see you there."
"Okay man, okay. Welcome back, my brother."

Day 13

The air along the Malecon tasted saltier at night than in daylight. Tonight, the waves sloshed gently against the wall, harmless and unthreatening. The spirit looked out across the water, squinting, as the children did, with hopes of catching a glimpse of the lights ninety miles to the North.

If only all those biographers could see this, could see him now. Not in Spain, among the matadors, or in Italy, among the vineyards; not even in Idaho, among the potatoes, which would have been his own bet, if past luck and Catholic justice had any say in the verdict. Initially, he spent a great deal of time trying to determine the nature of the assignment, to somehow discover the length of it, whether there were any expectations. As though researching for another novel, he sought out clues and details, only to learn nothing factually, and writing for no eager eyes but his own.

He learned they could hear him, when he wanted them to, and as proof of the Great One's true colors, he could consume and feel the glorious affects of alcohol. Impossibly, he had even managed physical interaction, at the ball game, watching the events unfold, letting his rage toward Raul and the Raul's of the world violently explode in an outburst of blame. Just as in life, he looked to the willing followers, not the Comandante, and laid responsibility at their feet. Their cowardice, and selfishness, was incredible.

Thoughts of a theme, revealing itself, kept him relatively sober since then, cautious not to show his hand or provoke Barbuda toward a rash, damaging action. Tonight, with this curious American returning to the city, all of the pieces were in place for a climactic finish. His fate tied into the outcome of the scenario, and though he still could not guess the intent, Barbuda's own dramatic emotional swings gave credence to the possibility of, finally, a power thrust against the Revolution.

All of these minor moves, all of these head games; it did not suit his personality. He was a man of action, condemned to services as a consigliore.

*   *   *   *

Gabrel chose the seat in the far corner, giving him vision of the entire, small bar. After the phone call, he went to a store he knew of nearby, buying a box of chocolates, and walking over, closer to the tourist section, by the Capitolo, to find a flower vendor and pick out a nice, healthy rose. He almost expected to arrive second, but entered the Hotel Lincoln to find the same cast of faces, the same girl on the same stool at the bar, whispering in the ear of a new friend, this one sounding Dutch. Gabrel stopped at the Bar Monserrate straight from the bus terminal, needing two mojitos to help him find the courage to call the old man. He finished a third after the call, now feeling swell and self-assured enough to stare at the blonde, knowing her prey could not see him, and as well could not see her, noticing, sending a wink his way.

Some time passed. Gabrel ordered a drink, finished it, and ordered another. He started mouthing words in the direction of the girl. She looked a lot better than the first time he had seen her, maybe because that instance, he had just managed a great round with Sandra, whereas this instance, he was anxious to get back into some action, the alcohol mixing with the time off and his hormones dominating his focus. She had a nice, full body, well-rounded in all the right places, probably with tighter skin, a firmer stomach a few years, maybe a few pregnancies ago, but still cutting a good figure. And what those years took away in looks, they repaid with savvy; he could see in her eye an accurate read of him, a desperate drunk happy to part with cash in exchange for a tumble, interested mostly in minimal effort.

That was the real truth of the deal, his desire to skip the courtship, to not have to earn the "honor" through symbolic, really meaningless, social gestures and conversation. He almost expected her to walk over to him, abandon her project, without any commotion or awkwardness. And maybe she would have, if Lazaro did not enter the bar at that moment, moving to Gabrel with arms outstretched, as though at a fond reunion.

Gabrel returned his smile, but the enthusiasm was forced. He had attributed Lazaro's lateness to a need to find, and prepare, Sandra. But she was not with him, and Lazaro could see the visible disappointment. That expression, those American eyes, unable to bluff, were the reason he waited, prolonged his entrance, and the reason he had Sandra standing by, but not there. He urged Gabrel to tell him of the places he went, the things he saw, extending the torture, listening to the mundane descriptions of spots he knew like the back of his hand, waiting for the American to find the guts to ask about the only thing on his mind. There was a rose, and a box of chocolates, set on top of his notebook, on the table next to the near-empty mojito glass. As though the days away were spent re-fortifying the barrier between them, repairing the holes in his morality. It was like he needed Lazaro to be the one to breach the subject. Only the devil could suggest the sin, to maintain a sense of propriety.

"Sandra could not be here." He shrugged. "Tomorrow, she can see you, I think, maybe."

"That's too bad," Gabrel tried to match Lazaro's ambivalence, but his eyes could not handle the task. "I don't have Old Samuel's phone number, do you? Can you call, let him know I'd like the room back?"

"I'm sorry, my friend, that won't work. Old Samuel is not around. I think he has gone to visit someone."

"What about Young Samuel?"

"I don't think you can stay there again. Sorry, man, but I don't think it will work out this time."

Lazaro was taking the high ground, re-establishing their business roles. He looked very at ease, his hands folded on the top kneecap of his crossed legs. Gabrel could imagine the experience in the ring, those confident eyes and that casual smile, laid back, knowing from the first bell whether he had the physical advantage—only sometimes the case—or if he would have to rely on his mental advantage—which more often than not was the key to his victory. He had spent a lifetime, the span of almost three of Sourdough's lives, sizing up opponents, finding their weaknesses and exposing them.

When he left Habana for Santa Clara, Gabrel did so realizing he was breaking all ties. That was why he did it; that was part of the technique. The time away dulled his sensitivity to their perceptions of him, and dulled his respect for Lazaro's capabilities and cutthroat agenda. Gabrel had looked down on him, tried to manipulate the old man, naively thinking he could get more from their arrangement than he had to give. But that was not how men like Lazaro survived into their sixties.

"Well, I guess I better go find a place to stay."

"I wish I could help you, man, really I do."

"Does Sandra have a phone number I could call?"

"Sorry, man, her mobile don't work. She call me when she can, she know to call. I will let her know you want to see her, I will give her the message."

Gabrel stood, steadying his balance with a hand on the table. He picked up the flower, and chocolates, and notebook, scooping them together under an arm. With the other arm he lifted the large, full back pack from the floor, swinging it over a shoulder, shifting his hip out to balance the weight. By now the blonde, and the Dutchman, were gone. He had not noticed her leaving, and now lusted for the easiness even more.

Gabrel nodded to Lazaro, stalking out of the bar, and Lazaro let him go. He had already made arrangements with the other casa particulars in the area. There was little question where the Americano would end up, the options in Centro limited as they were, and Old Samuel already somewhere in Mexico. There was also little question that the Americano would call him again, much as he would hate himself for doing it. The young stud's desire was practically oozing out of his pores, and in such predicaments, most men opt for the convenience of the known evil.

*   *   *   *

They did not speak much on the long trip back to the city, following the bus, picking up roadside riders, and stopping once for fuel. At the petrol station Raul placed a phone call, returning to the car a little less tense, but just as determined not to rebuild the bridge between them. Proximics, Fernando considered, usually worked in the opposite way; spending so much time together, so much time sitting next to each other, had a better chance of mending their relationship, that natural "in it together"-ness, than words, as there were not words, in the first place. He had dropped Raul off on a street corner, no hand shake or eye contact or thank you or threat. It had felt like their last chance, and they'd both chosen to let it pass. Fernando drove home, wondering and worrying what circumstances might bring them together again.

The answer was waiting in his apartment. Confirmation, in their round about way of communicating, that he had been paid, with apologies, but no explanation at the tardiness. The message was broken into two parts, and in their code there was no room for emphasis or dramatic pauses. Because of the nature of the correspondence, everything entered his head in the same monotone voice. "Payment in full completed. Clerical mistake on part of management."

And then, after some nonsense, included to ward off peering eyes, part two, "Enemy element presents new threat. Eliminate Operative Arrow as soon as possible. Direct report upon accomplishment." With that, after years of nothing, a short order to kill Raul, from faceless men in secret offices, who felt no cause to provide an explanation, and had ignored his request for clarification regarding the American, sent up prior to departing for Santa Clara.

In their way, they had answered it. Fernando sat down, untucking his shirt and unbuttoning the collar, slouching in the armchair. He wondered if he would feel any different, reading this, had they tried to patch things up, had Raul apologized or conceded, at least, that Fernando was not as dishonorably traitorous as he had emphatically implied. He also wondered, considering the giant web of informants and sources that he suspected existed, he playing a very minor role in the scheme, whether Raul's phone call, whether his own new guidance, had brought about this death sentence. He checked the message one more time. It had, in fact, arrived that day.

Funny, that they made sure to mention the pay, first, in the same message. Like they were suddenly afraid he might quit.

* * * *

This would be the first time in five years that Raul met face to face with his handler. The last occasion was merely an introduction, as the man was apparently replacing the old connection, whom Raul never actually met. In fact, based on the language of the correspondence, the directness, more assumption, less description this past year, he had good reason to believe the man waiting for him at the bar would be yet another new face, one that had not seen the need for an introduction, and had simply picked up where the last left off.

In all his years serving in the homeland espionage department of the government, Raul had been subjected to no formalities, received no benefits beyond standard rights as a citizen, and had never been offered a raise, promotion, or reprimand. He sometimes wondered if anyone ever retired, if the reason for new handlers had more to do with firings or congratulations, someone somewhere taking credit for Raul's hard work; or at least, for his exaggerated reports of minor incidents of little importance.

There was never a need for face-to-face, that was what worried him now. Great caution and care had been taken to create the parallel and supporting lines of communication, to maintain the surface separation between Raul and the official police. Maybe it was the stress and unknowns of the recent trip, or the hostility toward Fernando boiling in his stomach, but there seemed to him only one reason to meet his handler—this was the end of the road. Still, Raul turned the corner, walking into the bar. Better here, in a no name joint hidden half-way down an anonymous alley, head first, than crime scene photos of him strangled in his bed, the kind worthless policia could look at in their sweaty, stinky station house and sneer, "This fool never saw it coming." As he reached to open the door with his left hand, his right moved to his side, where a small, loaded pistol was holstered to the inner lining of his pants. He had a good knife, with a strong blade, strapped around his lower calf, under his sock, unnoticeable under his loose pants. Just the other day, in Bayamo, he'd nonchalantly reached down for it, pulling it out in front of Fernando to peel the rind off an orange. Not to scare him, just remind his old friend what he already knew.

He felt himself cramping, with butterflies, embarrassing as he stepped into the bar and found it empty. An old woman, not acting as a bartender, or a patron, but probably the wife or mother of the operator, looked up as he walked in. She reached into her apron, produced an envelope, set it on the bar, and left. Raul looked around again. The place was so small, and so poorly kept, had he not been directed to go there, he never would have guessed it an operating business, even by the low standards of establishments for locals. The relief and disappointment hit him simultaneously. No encounter, after all. Though he prepared for the worst, a part of him had secretly held out hope toward the promotion end of it, some kind of recognition. He had never really lost sight of the Americano, and even had Lazaro working for him now, to guarantee surveillance.

It was just a cheap envelope, hastily sealed. Raul tore it open and read the letter very quickly; the room was a little too dark, his imagination had messed with his head. There were so many ways to get information to him, ordering him on a scavenger hunt to a weird location away from the operative seemed counter-productive. And here it was, telling him, finally, to allow the scenario to unwind, then finalize the last phase. It was an issue of timeliness. They—whoever they were—wanted the matter concluded before sunrise. It was already past eight. They were so inefficient, he thought, folding the letter and stuffing it in his pocket.

* * * *

He had just descended the stairs from the second floor hostel when he first saw her, big hair bouncing up and down as she took short, quick steps, keeping her little body at the pace of the taller female friends in the group. The day thus far had been a rough, frustrating return to Habana, first with the disappointing hard-line techniques from Lazaro, and then, leaving in a huff, feeling the burden of his pack more than usual, he'd turned toward the tourist sector, the one place he knew he would not have to waste an hour stalking the streets to find one of the tiny hostel stickers in a welcoming window. The down sides to his move, turning into the first available place, a second floor with a nice common area, but a small room, were hammering his head now. Not only was the price twice what he'd paid Old Samuel—and where *was* Old Samuel?—but the old woman ran a tight ship, looking him over once, wagging a finger in his face and staring him down with eyes that probably had not flinched for very many things. "No girls," she said, then repeated again. "No girls, no chicas, not here, no aqui."

As she spoke, the occupant of the room across the hall from Gabrel's, a very large German man, a tuft of white hair atop a nearly spherical orb of a body, stepped out into the common area, a young thing obediently in tow. Still, the landlady did not flinch. "His wife," she explained. "They have papers to prove it."

All of that was behind him now, out in the open night air, with the good fortune of spotting the tasty little number and her entourage floating past as he emerged onto the calle. It was very uncommon to see local girls in their late-teens, early-twenties moving unescorted, and confidently. Gabrel decided to follow them, especially because they were walking a path away from Habana Viejo, which was the last place he wanted to be tonight.

They spied him after just a few blocks, stopped at a crosswalk, idly looking around and one of the taller girls noticing the foreigner noticing them, leaning down with an immediate report to her, always centered, clearly the ringleader. She swung the formation around toward him. The move was so alarmingly out of synch with city protocol, as he knew it, Gabrel stood his ground and awaited their approach. He was, after all, the turista. It was their aggressive necks exposed on the chopping block.

Her eyes were alien-big, but beautiful, complimented by well-positioned, long lashes, dominating a face with a tiny button nose and plump lips tied in a curious smirk. He realized she was not moving at their pace, but they were moving at hers, and the short, rapid gait was her natural way of walking. She smiled when she reached him; showing off a grand, perfect set of pearly white teeth.

"I am Yosnelly," she began, extending her hand for a shake and not giving him time to respond. "You want to go to club with us? You speak English, yes?"

"Um, yes-"

"I know English. I learn at university. You want to go to club with us? Come on."

With that she turned again, and they were moving at the old familiar clip. A university girl; the thought opened Gabrel's mind to a significant portion of the population that he had not even considered. Perhaps he'd been actively ignoring its presence all along. Yosnelly had no fear of policia because she had nothing to hide. She had no apprehension about approaching him, and inviting him along on their night out, because she was above the seediness; she did not come from the shadows, and had no intention of venturing there. He extended his stride to catch up to them. But when he did, they stopped, and Yosnelly swiveled, speaking more quickly and directly this time.

"You follow, okay? We walk, you can follow, but *behind*, maybe the best is other side of street, okay?" She made the universal sign he had seen before, the thumb and middle finger of one hand wrapped around the opposite wrist, then the move reversed. Handcuffs. "You understand me, yes? Is better this way. Okay, stay behind, vamos." She smiled again, a mouth straight from a toothpaste commercial, putting him at ease, if a little disappointed to be back in reality. Yosnelly was not afraid of the dogs, but that did not mean she was going to provoke them.

The party wound around the blocks, taking a course that seemed less than direct to Gabrel. They were tiptoeing along the border between Viejo and Centro, sticking to the main calles and avoiding the narrowest alleys, which also encouraged him. He kept a safe distance, and then some, lingering at times over a block behind them, so much so that twice Yosnelly stopped, and turned, to make sure he had not gotten lost. He ignored the similarities between this and the restaurant ritual conducted with Lazaro and Sandra. There were so many differences here; and fresh optimism for these final spurts of adventure on the island.

The group of girls finally halted at a pair of doors underneath a high, stone awning, just below the corner of a busy intersection, and across the street from a small, vacant park. The two doors were spread open, held in place by concrete blocks, serving as stops, and a rhythmic combination of Son music and hip-hop poured down a set of stairs, out onto the sidewalk. They lingered at the entrance, waiting for him, Yosnelly taking him by the forearm, a friendly, warm touch, and explaining the next set of instructions in a very methodical way; a pre-recorded message played before, many times.

"It cost five for each, five for each, but you cannot go in with us, or for you it will be more, maybe twenty. So five for each, but you go first, and we will wait to be sure you can get in. Now listen, because this is very important. When you get to the front of the line, you give the guy the five, and you do not let him say you must pay more. You insist, you must say that you know it is five, that you only have to pay five. Do not let him charge you more, because he will see you, and maybe ask for twenty. Go. Do not pay him anything but five. We will wait for you to get in."

Gabrel did as he was told, still thriving off of the buzz of the newness of the scenario, and giving her the entrance money without any ill will. Yosnelly could have suggested that she and her girlfriends go first, and provided a plausible reason, and he would have been totally screwed. At least now, if they split, and he made it inside, he could try to find new friends.

The line was long, and included few men, and no pale-skinned types. The girls looked fantastic; there was little doubt he would pay whatever the doorman insisted, as long as he had it in his pocket. Sourdough was second-guessing, regretting everything about his earlier experiences in the city, the value of that time. He watched as a young, sharply-dressed Cubano vehemently waved the five in his hand at the suited man behind the desk, pounded his fist on the table, then turned and stalked away, dejected, then returned and insisted again, before finally giving up, storming past Gabrel, back down the stairs to figure out a new plan for his night. As he approached the table, he sighed with premature defeat. If a native Spanish-speaker could not sell the argument, his less-than-basic skills and obvious foreign status held no chance.

Without a word, they took his money, ushering Gabrel inside.

* * * *

The dance club Rosario Castro, with a folk art, ceramic tile portrait of a stately old woman's profile above the inner entrance door, was but a link in a hidden chain of late-night groove spots providing a secluded, deviant atmosphere to the upper crust of foreign visitors and the premiere socialites, and girls, of the city. The place had not been mentioned in Gabrel's guidebook, because such broad advertising would attract a dangerously broad clientele. In Cuba, the old expression "all publicity is good publicity" did not pass translation.

The interior design had a modern chic to it, with bare brick walls intended to look rough, and tables set on the perimeter of a dance floor bathed in primary colors, beamed down from sky lights. He was a little early, but the place was not empty. Pin-up-worthy blondes and brunettes mingled in groups, idly twirling straws in mixed drinks, waiting for the crowd. There were other foreigners, too; a group of Chinese men, in business suits, circled around a table next to the dance floor. They had their own girls, and were sharing a bottle of rum among them. They did not look the sort to pass through a line, as he had. Like any decent club, the place must have a quiet rear entrance for the VIPs.

Yosnelly and her friends bumbled inside in no time, Gabrel automatically asking if she wanted a drink, Yosnelly, economically, suggesting that a bottle of rum would be too expensive, and if he just wanted to get them all a round of mojitos, that would be fine with the girls. Somewhere between ordering the drinks and paying, Gabrel's slow math realized that the drinks, combined, cost more than a bottle, and provided the group significantly less alcohol. He pointed this out to Yosnelly as the drinks were served, and she nodded matter of factly.

"Yes, yes, but after we finish the good drinks, then we can get the bottle, and everyone will have a great time!" She pinched his forearm and smiled up at him. She seemed even shorter now, standing next to him, inside. But she was such a bundle of constant energy, it was hard to look at the eyes and lips and bouncing afro of hair and not imagine acrobatic possibilities. So Gabrel just nodded, and tried to make conversation.

The place filled up quickly, and by eleven-thirty there was no need to move to the dance floor, as the walls reverberated with the rapid beats, and the girls all stood, responding in place. Most of them were in groups of friends, but even those with guys danced as individual shows. To the Cubans, these occasions were not about the kind of sloppy grinding Sourdough was used to seeing other places. These clubs were about display, full-body gyration, and many of the women looked overcome by spirits, hypnotically controlled as every inch of flesh moved at its own beat, turning the body into a thousand mini-quakes. Gabrel knew he could only move that way if he were being violently electrocuted. But there were no expectations of him, except that, when Yosnelly turned her head back, and looked up with a smile, his eyes were admiring her, and not one of the other magnificent specimens.

*   *   *   *

Lazaro kept looking down, at his feet, fidgeting around, and at his thin, old hands, grasping onto each other as if for security. The last thing he wanted to do was catch a glimpse of himself in one of the mirrors in the room, to serve as witness to this, his most humble hour. Raul stood over the little man in the chair, hands on his hips, contemplating whether or not to smack him, whether it would do any good.

"Why didn't you let him stay at the old man's place, Samuel's?"

"You told me to keep an eye on him. I have known that man for a long time." Lazaro risked a quick look up, than just as quickly jerked his head back toward the ground, in a submissive bow. "I have known that man for a long, long time. And I asked him about the American, and he told me he knew nothing. And I asked him again, and he reminded me that I took the American to him, not the other way around. He did not want trouble, so he left."

"The next thing you say better answer my question, I don't have time for this, old man."

"He never paid for the girl. Nothing. He paid nothing. He paid for the room, the price for the room, and nothing more. Like a jackal, the way he used her."

"And now you don't know where he is? I give you a very good deal, I tell you exactly what to do, and now I need to find him, and I cannot find him, because he did not pay you for a whore?" With a strong, well-angled kick, Raul knocked a leg from the wooden chair, and Lazaro fell to the floor in a fetal position. Then he looked over at the girl, still motionless, sitting upright on the bed, her back against the wall. Like the first time he'd seen her, she appeared entirely unafraid, unconcerned that she would be next on the floor. Her eyes briefly moved to Lazaro, and for that moment, showed a mild degree of sympathy, probably the most she knew how to muster. Then she looked back at Raul, almost bored, waiting on his next move. He stepped over the beaten boxer, striding toward the door of Lazaro's broken-down apartment without looking back. "You better hope he calls you again. You better hope this is the luckiest day of your life, or we are both in a big pile of shit."

* * * *

Fernando watched Raul exit the jinetero's slum apartment, turning and moving briskly toward the main calle. He looked frustrated, thinking, and genuinely nervous. Fernando felt the same way. It was evident Raul took great pride in his job, not simply because he was good at it, and had always been one of those people eager for the affection and approval of their superior, but also because of what his job was. Fernando had initially hated the American because the situation had seemed so unsettling, the young man represented a threat to his livelihood. Where there was resentment, he now considered, there should have been excitement. If he were really doing the job for patriotic reasons, if his motivation was as pure as he had insisted, an even match for Raul's, the sight of reinforcements, of a new, worthy addition to the effort, to the cause, would have been something to cheer and plan parades over. Instead, it was only self-preservation, and a pep talk from a hallucination, that had pushed him into action—and, shamefully, selfish action, at that.

Now he had flawlessly tracked a man who used to tell very good, dirty jokes, and was steadily gaining on him, unnoticed, with a switchblade knife tucked in the fist of his right hand, pressed against the inside of his wrist. Raul was focused on the evening's events, on the American, and had discarded Fernando as any real threat. Even if he was discovered mid-approach, there was no reason to think he could not ignore any hints of morality still inside him, long enough to methodically insert the blade deep into his old friend's chest, twisting and pushing and slipping his foot behind the backpedaling body, tripping him up, and letting the downward momentum extend his thrust. With any luck, Raul would be stone dead before they completed their tumble to the ground. And then he would run like hell.

The plan was fine, but age, and the long ride back from Bayamo, insisted on full commitment to the overall cause. By murdering Raul, all friendship aside, he would be permanently aligning himself with the anti-government effort, and there would be no going back. He would be acting in great faith, that the purpose of the American's arrival, that the value of his mission, and the mission of the anonymous men in the secret offices, was worth it. Because otherwise, if he lived to reflect on it, this would amount to an act of betrayal, against everything worth caring about, that would demand a merciless suicide.

Raul had stopped at a set of public telephones, just across from a small, poorly-lit park. There was a very narrow gap between buildings, only meters away from the phones. There were a few weathered faces on the benches, looking at nothing in particular. Fernando imagined how ridiculous this must seem, and for the first time considered that he was old enough to be a grandfather, and Raul, too. Two old men, servants to Kings they'd never met. More than anything, he hoped Raul would not turn around, he did not want to see the great passion leave his face. But at the last second, Raul did turn.

* * * *

Comandante Barbuda stood at the drawn curtains, looking out, through the thick, bullet-proof glass over the grounds, and the garden, in the rear of the complex. He bent his knees a little, doing mini-squats, letting the blood flow. He thought about getting out there, into that fresh night air, regardless the risk of being spotted, his vastly improved condition unfortunately leaked and publicized. No, he would fight the urge; it was worth waiting. He had just put the finishing touches on the note cards he would use in the speech. The necessary personnel were notified, so that, like clockwork, the factories and businesses would close, the children released from school, and the policia in place to effortlessly guide the mob of mid-day citizens toward the public square, for what had been halfheartedly announced as a ground-breaking ceremony for a new library; an event of little importance.

When they saw the security force in place, the familiar caravan of shiny, black SUVs and Mercedes Benzes, a wave of excitement, a buzz of anticipation, would sweep across them. And then, before the journalists could fumble for their telephones, or send out urgent, high-priority messages, without even an emcee to frame the event and make an introduction, he would appear, after so many rumors, so many write-offs, and he would speak directly to the children, and the citizens, ignoring the cameras and photographers, keeping the international misfits out of the speech, and out of his mind. He wanted to make it clear, he was returning for his people, and his full-recovery was not a personal victory, but a national triumph.

Barbuda had thought about trimming his beard a little more, then decided to leave it as it was; rough, messy, as though he had too many things on his mind to worry about his looks, which was true. And also, sending the message that his supporters certainly wanted to see him healthy, and would not be concerned one way or the other over the shape and order of the facial hair. What mattered was that it was still there, still growing as it pleased. That's what would whip them into a roaring cheer.

He listened as the grandfather clock, a gift from another nation's leader, whose own legacy had long ago drifted from the average man's memory, chimed its hourly sound. It was midnight. By sunrise, his longtime adversary would once again be scratching its collective head, second-guessing its narrow-minded ambition, and, hopefully, deciding to forgo any further paltry stabs at playing Goliath.

Barbuda looked across the broad complex, at the city lights blurred beyond the garden. This was not their land. It would never be their land, never again. He thought about the spirit, amused as he imagined the preferable flavor of their next conversation.

*   *   *   *

Perhaps by design, to complete the intensity of the atmosphere, the Rosario Castro club did not provide much ventilation, and soon the firm, fit, gyrating bodies were covered in a healthy, erotic film of sweat, mixed into cosmetic creams and touches of perfume. The DJ showed no mercy, no hints of slowing the pace or allowing the lesser dancers time to catch their breath. And the girls were up to the task, meeting with approving, devious grins from the Chinese businessman, their suit jackets by now removed, ties loosened, and the official itinerary discarded like an empty bottle tossed with abandon to the floor.

Gabrel's own thrill was fading, even as he tried to maintain it by keeping up a strong alcoholic buzz. The problem was Yosnelly. At first, her energy and confidence and take-charge approach, polar opposite of Sandra, wowed him. But as the evening progressed, her expectation that Gabrel would happily fund the night for everyone proved to be the white elephant in the club.

Insisting that she could get a better price than the bartender would give him, Yosnelly extended an open palm, her other hand venturing to a cozy spot along his hip. But when she returned with more drinks, she brought back no change. It was also more than annoying that, of the select handful of Cubano males in attendance, every one of them knew her, received a wave from her, and moved to her for a hug and a peck on the cheek. This would not have bothered him so much if they did not so completely ignore him, and if they had paid any attention to the other girls in the group. But the only one friendly and fully accessible to them was Yosnelly. And she was accessible to them all.

Not that she ignored Gabrel. She would occasionally turn to dance face-on with him, or help guide his hands to generous locations along her hips and lower pelvis. She enjoyed backing into him, bumping in a tease grind, and seemed to grow more familiar the more that she drank. Yosnelly was getting drunk, and so were her friends. Sourdough's gamble was whether he had enough cash left in his pocket to get them through the whole night. If his funds fell short, there was little question now, so would his chances of getting laid.

It was that last thought which brought Gabrel back to himself. He loosened his grip on Yosnelly, letting her float forward a step, looking out over the crowd. The transition occurred so seamlessly, he had not noticed. First, he followed her, and paid as she directed, believing it a small preliminary step toward finally engaging a true jewel of the island; a young lady with the mind, heart, and tenacity to be a part of a bold future, a flower representative of the finest, growing wild, out on the mountainside. Now, no better than the businessmen up front, he had fallen into the worst caricature of himself; the boozed monster prowling for self-serving, fleeting gluttonous purposes. The pangs of bitterness he'd been suppressing, toward Yosnelly as she brought more and more friends into the fray, sponsoring their evening on Gabrel's account, also felt newly unfair. None of this was her fault, really. He had hoped for purity when all signs indicated shrewd craftiness. She was methodically milking him of everything she could get, a University girl whose higher education did not denounce hustling, but fostered and refined the skill set. Yosnelly did not need a Lazaro. She was the beauty, and the boxer, wrapped in one capable bundle.

Gabrel realized he needed to go. Nothing worthwhile could be achieved there, just another event produced by shallow intentions and near-sighted lust. Yosnelly, suddenly aware of the space between them, backed herself up again, to the steady beats of the music. Gabrel allowed her to rub into him, close enough to whisper in her ear that he needed to go to the restroom. It was located on the other side of the dance floor, and the easiest way there was to move to the wall and slide alongside it, which he did, to the exit door half-way, not turning to check if she was watching, knowing only that if she were, she was smart enough to realize if she could not catch him by the foot of the stairs, there could be no pursuit out into the street. Such a scene did not happen in Habana.

*   *   *   *

Their struggle was short, and ugly. Raul had timed his move well, and though he lacked the swiftness of a top-rate professional, he sprung into action fully confident that Fernando had no hope of matching blows. In his initial spin, having monitored the approach all the way, he used an old military disarming trick, seizing firm control of Fernando's wrist, twisting it sharply, locking the muscles and forcing his hand to give up the blade, which fell to the ground with a mild clinking sound. Locking the aged adversary's elbow, Raul pulled him deep into the narrow, pitch black space between the two buildings, next to the public phones. He was backing up in good faith that he would not trip, and with a superior reach, held Fernando submissively in a mighty choke hold. He raised his knee as powerfully as he could, burying it in the stomach, then let go his hold, lurching for the knife tucked into his sock, and bringing it up at the last second, as Fernando was falling into him with a desperate rush of a counterattack.

Raul fell to both knees for stability, lifting his opponent's full body weight from the ground for an instant, keeping the knife inserted, using his underneath position for leverage, steadily jerking the blade along, extending the size of the insertion, careful not to take it out and somehow lose the advantage. Fernando was completely lifeless within a minute, and even in the thick darkness, the blood, spilling everywhere, held a glimmer. It poured from him like aged port wine out of a busted cask, onto the ground, and the walls isolating them from view. Raul suddenly realized he was still extending the insertion, accomplishing nothing but the further staining of his own clothes.

Gradually shifting himself to the side, Raul let the body slip off of his shoulder, and leaned against the wall looking down at it, trying to catch his breath. His chest hurt, a lot, and he anxiously ran his fingers over his entire upper torso, checking for a wound he did not realize he had sustained.

There was no where to go, no way to really get there without being noticed. Even the most gullible policia, or the greediest, could not turn a blind eye, in the center of the city, to a man in blood-soaked clothes. His chest felt tightly constricted, breathing a challenge, and his head throbbing roughly around his temples and eyes, as though Fernando had landed some roundhouses, and the adrenaline rush delayed the impact of the shots.

Raul realized he had only one option: Lazaro. He was close, he had extra clothes, and hopefully he was intimidated enough at this point to act with rapid purpose. He reached into his pocket for his cell phone, looking down at Fernando, and noticing, for the first time, the bloodied envelope folded and tucked in his old drinking buddy's back pants pocket.

* * * *

The unsure knock on the door startled Lazaro, and reminded him briefly of times, between rounds, when due to the daze of a stiff combination, or the monotony of his trainer's instructions, his mind had floated away from the moment, but jerked back to reality due to the abrupt, high-pitched singing of the timekeeper's bell.

Sandra was not sure why she did, but she leapt from the bed and hurried toward the door, peering through the keyhole and feeling a jolt like no other. She sprang back toward the mattress, diving onto it face first. Something in her bounce, a shine in the eye, gave new life to Lazaro. It was not his nature to expect or plan on miracles. But he opened the door to find the Americano, clothes sweaty and smelling of spilled drinks, standing there, desperate, begging to be put down on the canvas.

Lazaro quickly reverted to his old persona, welcoming the boy as a guest, the old brotherly pat, guiding him to the back portion of the apartment, where Sandra still had her head, and her smile, buried in a pillow. She was wearing a skimpy top, and a short, tight, baby blue mini-skirt. Lazaro jokingly, wearing his devilish grin, motioned for Gabrel to give her a playful slap on her bottom.

Instead he fell down on the bed beside her, twisting her around by the waist so she lay there, facing him, beaming ecstatic sunshine out of her eyes.

Lazaro had an urgent phone call to make, but was apprehensive about leaving them alone, and risking coming back to find Sandra had stubbornly, again, capsized the situation. Her enthusiasm seemed genuine, and the Americano looked primed for immediate gratification. Abbreviated small talk sufficed, Lazaro suggesting he step out for some air, Gabrel replying with a compromising suggestion that they finally do that disco night, all of them together, maybe in an hour, if that wasn't too late. The men exchanged nods, and Lazaro moved to the door, mentioning that he'd be locking it behind him, and nobody could get in unless they let them. Sandra, of course, knew that this was not true, but it seemed no reason to meddle with the mood. As soon as the door closed, they tore into each other, mutually undistracted for the first time.

*   *   *   *

Raul carefully unfolded the envelope, sliding out the letter and opening it to read. The blood had got to it, the paper damp, the writing in some places smeared. Raul's hands were no help, and wiping them off on his pants made little improvement. He knew he needed to get out of there, get out of that situation, as quickly as possible. But first he would read the letter.

Initially, it seemed to be nothing but a nonsensical note, from a relative in Spain. But the quality of paper was poor, the small crisp envelope had a familiar texture, and the layout of the letter, the uneven font, from a typewriter instead of a computer, and the spacing between paragraphs, the unpunctuated sentences, pointed to an undeniable source. This was the directive he had been told about, when he made the phone call to his handler, from the gas station along the highway. This was the letter from his people, meant to convince Fernando it was from *his*, taking advantage of the tip they had confirmed, that the opposition decided to break ties with their non-citizen field rats.

This was definitely that letter, Raul thought as he read over it, then over it again, and a third time, remembering what the coded message over the telephone had been, making sure he understood it correctly, that Fernando would be directed to terminate the young American, with a brief, but decent enough explanation that the operative had been instructed to abort the mission, but had disregarded the order, gone renegade, and was now posing an unchecked, uncontrolled threat of volcanic proportions. Raul scanned the letter again. They had used their understanding of the American encryption, a system he had only limited experience decoding. Finally, he found the word he was looking for, and his chest constricted even tighter. It felt like a nail being driven into his sternum, as he realized what he was looking at.

They had directed Fernando to terminate Raul, not the American. With an excuse of the threat of the Cuban agent compromising the mission, not the explanation of the mission cancellation, as it had been explained to him. Raul was led to think Fernando would follow him to find the American, then, at Raul's failure, complete the dirty work himself, leaving the faceless folks in offices around Washington, D.C., to massage their skulls and point fingers at each other, ultimately writing the plan's failure off to vengeance on the part of a bitter foreign national, who never was worth his spot on the payroll in the first place.

So what could this mean, his managers wanting him dead? That they knew his reports had been something less than full? That, along with this, they no longer considered the American a threat? Or … he knew it, now that he was having a heart attack … were they, those who never introduced themselves, who shuffled jobs and got promotions … finally revealing their self-serving allegiances? A coup, set in motion, collaborated with the Great Enemy, and with he, Raul, old and now a murderer of his closest friend, the only one in position to block their move?

He fumbled for his cell phone, which he finally realized had been ringing. It was Lazaro, and he was standing a half-block away.

* * * *

Lazaro rushed to the scene, fast as his bad hip could handle. He conducted a quick scan as he turned into the narrow corridor; there were no policia immediately around, only others, like him, who had no intention of getting involved in something that was none of their immediate business, and could not possibly be worth getting hauled to a station over.

It was darker than he had expected, barely any moonlight or street light filtering down from above. Lazaro could hear Raul breathing, gasping, unsteady and agitated, and could see him, on one knee, his shoulder and side leaning heavily on the wall, supporting his weight. Only when he reached him did Lazaro finally notice the other body, smelling it first, sensing its position by the way Raul knelt off to the edge of it. There was a lot of blood, and the man was very much past dead.

The evening had been swinging dramatically, and Lazaro felt a little lightheaded. Then the dizziness went away, and he rotated his shoulders back, stiffening his posture, puffing out his chest cavity, and looking down, at the body, the knife to the side of it, the paper crumpled into a ball in Raul's fist, and that fist tucked tightly against his chest, trying to softly pound it, the way a man might smack a television and hope it improved the reception.

"Wha' happen here?"

"Listen ... I need some fresh clothes ..." Raul sounded weak, finished. Lazaro squatted down, and picked up the knife. "That American is going to murder Comandante ... and they are going to let him ... they want him to do it ..."

Everything about the situation suggested matters far above Lazaro's world. Even in it, among the other weeds and vermin, he had not seen a murder, a dead body hidden just out of public view, in more than ten years. Raul certainly held some kind of position of importance in the regime, and the body, face down, continuing to spill a sea of blood in all directions, certainly represented some sort of opposition. Lazaro managed a thoughtful smirk, his eyes glazing over in their old pre-fight way. If this dying murderer was not delirious, the fate of the island, the future of this way of living, may have been brought down by an angel, and placed in his lap.

"I need some fresh clothes ... we need to find the American right away ... I think I know where we can start looking ..."

"Yes, me too. I think I know where he is." Lazaro carefully took hold of the tuft of hair atop Raul's head, lifting it skyward and very precisely pointing the knife into the man's neck, just above the shirt collar, intending to slice through the windpipe, across to the far ear, and to make sure to guide the head and body down on top of the other, so it would not fall on him, so he would not have to worry about looking suspicious as he darted back out of the corridor. But as Raul's eyes widened, then rolled, and his body began to spasm, Lazaro let go, stepping back. The last convulsions rippled through the government agent, and he flapped forward, on top of his old chess partner.

Keeping his face down, Lazaro took a long, roundabout route back to his apartment. There was no need to cut them short, no longer any need to hurry.

* * * *

He gauged the time too generously, playing the game and knocking, to wait for Sandra to open it, and instead having it opened by the American, already dressed and on his way out. He greeted Lazaro with a smile, but the submissive desperation was gone from his face, his animal urges now satisfied and his need for the old man depleted. Sandra sat on the side of the bed in the far room, he could see her legs dangling off of the mattress, her head and shoulders and arms as she sat hunched forward, elbows on knees, and looked to have some money in her hand.

Lazaro smiled, his friendly face, at the Americano. "We still going to the disco, man?"

"Yeah, yeah, of course." He took a step to the side, to get by Lazaro and complete his exit. "I'm going first, I will be inside. I gave Sandra entrance money. You know, don't want any trouble. Can you walk her there for me?"

Lazaro nodded. He realized he was still a little stunned by what he had seen in the alley, still remembering Raul's last words and mulling them over for value, for a game plan to suit his own needs. His mind had been occupied with regret, not for the lost gym possibility, but over allowing Raul's bad heart to finish him, instead of stealing the glory with a solid roundhouse combination, to repay the earlier insult. He had not determined what to do with the Americano. The young man was gone before Lazaro had time to react, leaving him to turn back to Sandra for an explanation.

She had a new fire in those normally subdued eyes. He could see, as he approached, that she only had a five in her hand. "What's that?" he asked, already knowing.

"It's for me. He only gave me enough for one."

"He finished early, very fast?"

Sandra shook her head, looking at the floor. "He did not finish."

"You tell him you need enough for both of us?"

"No."

"You remind him he never pay for you last time?"

"No."

"You expect me to walk you, through the dirt and the trash out there, to walk you to the disco, then come back here and sit and wait like an old woman? For what? For you to call and summons me to go and walk you back again?"

Lazaro could see in her face new empowerment. She did not keep her gaze on the floor, but looked up at him. Perhaps she thought the worst he would do was beat her again, perhaps she did not think him capable of worse. Perhaps she thought she was in love, which angered him even more, the way young girls gleefully, foolishly cast their lots with strangers, anxious to abandon their proven providers.

He had let Raul die because the man, and the men he represented, disgusted Lazaro. He hated them bitterly, enough to willingly throw his future into unknown chaos if it meant those bastards finally getting their overdue punishments. Everything he had become was a result of his reaction to them, and they never stopped badgering, never stopped swinging away, keeping him on the defensive. He survived, and would keep on surviving, because he was a fighter; a smarter, craftier fighter than all of them. But that did not lessen his hatred of their hollow slogans, their hypocritical morals.

And as he reached for the money, ripping it from Sandra's hand, tossing her toward the closet, filled with her few changes of clothes, telling her to get out, for good, forever, Lazaro realized he loathed the Americano just as much. For reasons so similar, for the shared responsibility of the predicament, and the willingness to deepen the wound by coming here, now, and daring to act so innocent. Lazaro felt explosive, totally drained and totally primed. He could see all of his opponents at once, for the first time. All of them in the ring, all of them backing him into the corner, working together to pound on him, synchronizing their blows, pounding and pounding, he could see them all at once.

* * * *

The discotheque where Gabrel sat, at the bar with a mojito, waiting for Sandra, was the same one, he realized, Lazaro had stopped at that first night. This was the place where he had approached the door man and asked about the hours, giving Sourdough a chance to lean in toward the pretty girl, and drunkenly cut to the chase. It was a very different place from the Rosario Castro, where, by now, Yosnelly had probably found a new sponsor, one happy to fill the sugar daddy role. Afterall, that's why most of them were there. In so many ways, it was more his fault than hers; he was the one breaking the expectations of the roles.

This place was filled with Cuban men, and the male turistas present had to enter through the front door, just like everybody else. There was good music, and the interior maintained a sophisticated look, but the room could not hide its rough side. A half-hour passed, which meant either she was not coming, or Lazaro had another southpaw hook in his satchel of tricks. Done with his drink, and not liking not knowing, Gabrel moved back to the door, dipping out onto the street.

He spotted her right away, the sight so peculiar, every set of eyes, from the door man to the policia to the taxi drivers, was probably watching. Sandra was walking, slowly, down the very center of the calle. It was a late hour, but there was still traffic, yet she stayed centered, preferring the danger of avoiding speeding cars to the annoyance of dodging shady men. In each hand she carried a white plastic bag, the kind you might get at a grocery store checkout, and the bags were stuffed with clothes, shoes, earrings, and the like. The plastic stretched under the contents, and Sandra struggled under the weight. But she maintained her steady walk, and spotted Sourdough, moving to meet her.

"What happened? What are you doing?"
"Lazaro." She shook her head.
"Where are you going?"
"Mi casa. Yo regresso."
"You are coming back?"
"Si."
"To the disco?"
"Si."
"You want me to go with you?"
"No."
"You want me to wait for you at the disco?"
"Si."
"Do you have the money?"
"No. Lazaro."

He wanted to reach for the bags, or at least give her a hug, but they were the center of everyone's attention by now, and he could see in her eyes a pleading not to do anything. As she stepped past him, turning toward the street running past the Hotel Lincoln, toward the poor, decrepit housing at the heart of Habana Centro, she promised over her shoulder that she would return, promised it would only take twenty minutes. One of the policia stood at that corner, facing Gabrel, as though he were screening people from walking in that direction. He let Sandra pass, watching her, as they all did, shamelessly.

To Gabrel it was clear, this was out of the ordinary. Something very significant was happening; in the last hour, Sandra's life had dramatically changed. Whether for better or worse was not an argument to be left to philosophers, but a determination she would have to sort out for herself. He had no reason to expect her to be back. The hour was late, and her priorities, now, could not realistically include a few more moments with him. Gabrel re-entered the disco, returning to his stool at the bar. Much as he did not want it to, guilt dominated his thoughts. He questioned his motives, considered the degree of damage it now seemed he had causelessly inflicted.

His self-pity was interrupted by one of the club's bouncers, tapping him on the shoulder and gesturing toward the glass window by the entrance, where Lazaro was standing, waving him out, with a new young girl waiting by his side.

* * * *

Gabrel went out to meet him. Neither had anything to hide any longer, nor any reason to hold back real feelings. Lazaro could see the disgust, the desire to hit him, in the Americano's eyes. Gabrel could see, in the thin grin and cocked-back head, that Lazaro was daring him to do it. But the old man's eyes blinked first, and in his pupils was the desperation of a player who'd lost his queen, and was trying to survive on pawns.

"Sandra is gone," Lazaro began, aware of the earlier scene. He hoped, somehow, from liquor or animal lust or practicality, Sourdough would be willing to let bygones be bygones, and just wanted laid one more time before he left the island. "She no good, no good. Here, here is Daisy, very good girl for you."

Gabrel did not even look at her. "Where does Sandra live?"

"She is gone, man, she not come back. Sandra will not come back." The Americano looked over in the direction of the street. The policia had moved, was smoking a cigarette with a friend on the other side of the calle. Lazaro continued to force his case. "She go to her husband, man. She have husband, and baby. I am telling you, man, Sandra no good for you, she not come back. Daisy, here, very good, very young-"

Gabrel stepped past him, and moved to the corner. Lazaro grabbed the girl by the arm and pulled her along in pursuit. She was wearing some flimsy high heels, and Lazaro, with his old limp, fared no better. Gabrel was walking hurriedly, frantically, scanning the windows of the buildings for lights, for movement, for generous faces who might know her, or know where she lived. He was already a block ahead by the time Lazaro rounded the corner off of the main calle, and the gap between them was expanding. Still, he persisted, pulling the girl along, yelling out, knowing the effort was wasted, but at the least wanting to see, at the end of this ridiculous hunt, that the Americano would know his effort, too, was for nothing. "She not come back, man. Sandra is nothing, man! She don't care about nothing!"

Gabrel ambled on. He had never walked these streets before, never been so deep in Habana Centro. There was nothing there but crowded, old housing, a few closed stores that looked like they offered very limited, low-grade products. If this city was the heart of the country, this spot was the weakest valve in the organ, whose ever-imminent collapse might trigger the domino failure of the entire body. There were no policia, and very few street lights. The darkness disoriented him. But looking over his shoulder, and seeing the old, bastard boxer, still yelling, still dragging the girl along, propelled Gabrel onward. He walked another block, with no sign of Sandra, then turned down, looping his route to bring him back up a different calle, ending near the discotheque. He had no desire to cross paths with Lazaro again, ever. Especially since it seemed he was right, she was gone. On the walk back, Gabrel tormented himself over the misfires and failures, with the sunrise only a few hours off.

It was easy to recognize the Calle Zapata, lit up, with periodically passing old cars, street sounds and policia lingering, maintaining a security net to keep drunken turistas from waking in the wrong place, and from opportunistic locals from persuading them toward amoral offerings. The policia looked at him, a little curious, maybe wanting to ask what he was doing in that neighborhood at such a late hour, but not wanting to embarrass themselves by showing their weak English. As Gabrel came back to the main street, he resolved to have a last drink in the disco—one last mojito—and then see how the sunrise looked around the Malecon, before crawling back to the unused casa particular, claiming his bag, and finding a taxi for an airport run.

She was standing out on the street, as before, now in a modest, simple blue dress, less suggestive than the mini skirt and low-cut top she had on earlier. She was standing there, twirling in anxious circles, looking for him and looking out for Lazaro, and fully aware of the hungry eyes of the taxi drivers, doormen, and policia, and looking beautiful in the glow of the streetlights, and terrified that he had left, and was gone, and was not coming back. When she saw him, she moved uninhibited, straight and steady to him, wrapping her bare arms around his neck and kissing him, there, in the center of the street, the move shocking Gabrel as much as it thrilled him. She tucked her arm into his, spinning to his side and nodding toward the entrance to the club. They needed to get in before one of the onlookers summoned the guts to react. And certainly before Lazaro found his way back.

*   *   *   *

Sandra looked around, unable to hide or control her smile, as though she had never been inside the place before. Considering its proximity to her world, that seemed impossible. More likely, Gabrel considered, it was her first time there without a chaperon. This was possibly the first genuine date of her young life.

A waiter guided them to a table, and Gabrel asked what she wanted to drink. Sandra looked around again, at the high-end girls, the sharp-dressed men, the mixed drink glasses, leather purses, and jewelry. Then she ordered the cheapest can of beer Gabrel knew of in the city, the brand he bought at the small stores, to take to Old Samuel's, to share with her in their room. The mesero brought them glasses, but they drank straight from the can; it tasted cold and fantastic.

Sandra liked to dance, just as Gabrel had always been told. She spun and stepped gracefully, a clear contrast from Sourdough's careless footwork and inexperienced swaying. Still, she followed his amateur lead, her smile ever-present, her eyes mostly fixed on the screen to the side of the dance floor, where projected electronic images of funny cartoon characters and bouncing shapes complimented the rhythm of the sounds. After a few songs she showed mercy on him, they took a break from the floor and returned to their seats.

Gabrel and Sandra repeated the rotation for an hour, dancing a few songs, resting a spell, finishing a can of beer and ordering another, returning to the dance floor. Her eyes were on everything, the people, the video screen, the DJ, and the Americano. His eyes were only on her, awestruck by her enjoyment, by the simple fact she was sitting there, with him, after the prospect had seemed so lost. Gabrel knew their time was short; the club would only stay open a little while longer. Lazaro's apartment was out of the question and so, too, was the casa particular; with the old lady's policy, the night did not need more conflict. This was why he felt so deeply saddened when she gestured for them to leave, her own expression very fulfilled, reminding him of the morning he'd left for the bus terminal, and her uncaring, finished demeanor in the elevator from Old Samuel's apartment.

But exiting the dance club, she tucked her arm inside his again, the inner part of her elbow locked to his own, her posture perfect and her stare straight ahead as she steered him, by the arm, to the corner of the block, and turned them down the side street where Gabrel had ventured in search of her. The policia stood with his arms crossed just a few meters away, with nothing to do but stare at them, no thoughts in his mind but his job description. He took a step toward them, and Gabrel's stomach churned. Then Sandra turned her head, freezing the man with her stare, stripping him of whatever machismo-fueled confidence normally supported him in his duties. They passed, unobstructed, and continued for quite some distance before turning, then again, and arriving at an apartment building that looked like every other.

Sandra had a key tucked into a space in her dress. She opened the outer gate, leading Gabrel inside with a finger to her lips, up a flight of stairs, and carefully, quietly, creeping, guiding him by the hand, into her abuelita's apartment, around the sparse furniture in the dark living area, and back to her bedroom, at the end of a short, narrow hall. Inside, on the bed, Gabrel recognized the two white plastic bags, still packed with her clothes and belongings from Lazaro's. As he looked around, removing his shoes, he realized there were very few other possessions.

∗   ∗   ∗   ∗

The sheets of the queen-sized bed, which was caved in the center from wear and no box-spring support, were not quite large enough for the mattress, barely reaching and covering the corners, and leaving some spots showing. Sandra's first move was to adjust this, neatly and carefully pulling the bottom sheet taut, scanning the perimeter frame and ensuring it looked respectably cared for before slipping out of her dress and shoes, down to a simple red thong piece. Then she moved the bags of clothes into an otherwise bare, old wooden stand-alone closet, and stood, shifting her weight to favor a leg, crossing her arms in front of her chest, and watching the Americano. He walked the room slowly, as though it were a museum, but with a generous, rather than critical, eye. First to the dolls—there were two of them, one with a ceramic face, the other traditional, made of patchwork fabric, that looked like it had spent many nights stuffed tightly into Sandra's embrace. Then to the photos—there were two of them, as well. Both had been taken the same night, and not long ago, and in an outfit combination, jeans and a tight, pink shirt, Gabrel had seen Sandra wearing. She posed with a smile in one, biting into a piece of pizza in the other. Perhaps taken by Lazaro, perhaps snapped at his direction as he stood alongside the photographer. Somehow, they bore his mark, though she alone was framed.

He, too, undressed, sitting carefully on the other side of the bed, trying not to disturb the lay of the sheets. There was a set of drawers to his right, between him and the window. Sandra could see him deciding what was and was not appropriate, what she wanted and did not want to show him. The truth was, she wanted to show him everything, and she climbed across him, her bodyweight resting on his lap as she pulled open the lower of the two drawers, revealing a collection of four or five wigs, much to her delight. She laughed as she modeled them, a color range from blonde to platinum to purple, and laughed even more as he modeled them after her.

Then Sandra stood to turn out the ceiling light, to slide out of the underpants, and the Americano slid under the top blanket, holding it up for her to join him. For the first time, he did not rummage in his pockets for a condom, did not give it to her to put on. For the first time, she let herself think about it, about exactly what was happening and nothing else, not what happened earlier, not about tomorrow, and not about paint chips falling from the ceiling.

Her gestures, her openness, annihilated Gabrel. Much as he wanted control of the situation, he had no hope of holding it.

Day 14

Afterwards, in the hour of predawn darkness, then on a little longer, they slept, Sandra with her head on his chest and her arm across it, Gabrel with his eyes mostly open, his thoughts dominated by indecision over how and when to leave. Despite the brevity of the actual intercourse, the atmosphere and details lifted him to an unexplored feeling of content. Now, that morning, he had to leave the island. Emotional summits did not come at any higher elevations.

When the moment seemed right, when the pattern of her breathing changed, signaling she might be awake, he shifted her weight, and she let him slide out from underneath. Gabrel stood, and was entirely dressed, down to the sandals, within a minute. Most of his money was gone, spent on drinks for Yosnelly and her friends. A part of him wanted to give her what was left; a part of Sandra sensed this, and she said a little prayer in her mind, pleading to the gods that he not.

Saying nothing, Gabrel sat down beside her body, still under the top sheet. He reached for his neck, loosening the hemp chord that held the pewter medallion, removing it. Carefully he slipped it over her bulky hair, retightening the band to a good fit, nodding in approval of its position. Then he kissed her, and Sandra stood, reaching for a towel hanging on the doorknob, fitting it around her torso and tucking it securely under an armpit.

She led him to the front door of the apartment, through the living area quietly, her abuelita still peacefully asleep. Gabrel kissed her again, and she opened the door, his hands still wrapped affectionately around her waist. The door directly across the hall was opening at the same moment, an old man letting his grade-school granddaughter, in her clean, light-purple uniform, go off to her classes. On a self-conscious impulse, Gabrel let go of Sandra, blowing her another kiss as he stepped away, out the door, and kept waving as he followed the schoolgirl down the stairs to the first floor of the building. Once he was out of view, Gabrel turned his attention to the exit, his thoughts to an expedient route to the casa particular, and the likely flight times back to Mexico City. And Sandra closed her door.

* * * *

The convoy of shiny, black, bulletproof cars raced through the city, on a tight schedule. Policia barricades were only now setting up, and in an hour traffic would be at a standstill, all those able-bodied encouraged to follow the throngs to the gathering, to witness for themselves an event of national and historic significance. Soon the radio station DJ's would be handed the memorandums, soon the school principals would be called and informed. By then the turistas would be reaching for cameras, the foreign journalists scrambling for pens and palm pilots, and the international agencies on their telephones and internet connections, rushing to inform their sponsors and employers. They had nothing to report but rumor; nothing to fuel their efforts but speculation. Some would disregard the commotion as yet another false alarm. Tomorrow, sweating, they would have to explain why they missed it.

The car telephone rang, an assistant answered, then held the receiver out for Comandante Barbuda, who pulled it eagerly to his ear. He had expected verification at morning breakfast, but instead received only news of no news. He had finished his meal, and pushed on with the plans.

"Si? Que?"

He was a man of extraordinary character and resolve; the kind who did not just take bad news in stride, but used it to motivate him forward, more determined than before. Reminding himself of this, it was easy to keep his hand steady holding the phone, to nod as he listened, his expression and breathing unchanged, and to hand the phone nonchalantly back to the assistant and gesture for it to be hung up. He could sense that the spirit was with him, and though this agitated him, he held his poise.

"Bad news from the front?" The spirit sounded coy, and was clearly already aware.

"Some dead bodies, murder in the night."

"But not the one you were expecting, eh?"

"No, not the one I expected."

Barbuda sighed, and realized he had been holding his breath. He still felt strong. "No reason to adjust the agenda."

"Sadly, you're right about that. Pity of it is, he's going to miss your fine speech. He's in a taxi right now, on his way to the airport." He could see Barbuda's surprise, and anger, and continued. "Not responsible for either one of those deaths, you should know. Spent the night with a young girl, pretty thing, first at a club, then in her bed. He woke, and he left, and in about an hour his flight will take off."

"Are you telling me they have another operative here?"

"No. I'm telling you, they don't have anyone here."

Barbuda could feel his perspiration, leaking through crevices in his uniform. He could feel the impact in his stomach, a side cramp, and legs suddenly lifeless, which would have given out from under him had he been standing as the spirit spoke. He pressed the intercom button.

"Stop here."

He pressed it again, leaning into the speaker.

"Stop here! I need some air! I want to take to the air!"

The driver slammed on the brakes like a man with a gun to his head, swerving to the side of the road, out of line. The three security vehicles in front kept going around the turn, and the three behind swerved, but sped on as well. All of the drivers had been strictly instructed not to brake, and none of them knew who sat on the other side of the solid, bulletproof divider. They just knew that orders were to be followed, until new orders superseded.

Barbuda gestured for the assistant, who looked young, confused, and scared, to open the door and get out of his way. He put his boot down outside of the car, carefully and firmly, holding the door and frame to lift himself out of the seat, and into the air. A crowd was gathering, curious, admiring the fancy vehicle, but cautious not to get too close to it. When he stood, and his face looked out at them, it was met by silent shock; measured disbelief. Many would later remark, in interviews, that it was the least-accurate decoy of the man they had ever seen passed off. By now the soldier in the front passenger seat, and the driver, were both opening their doors, reaching for weapons, and hustling out to perimeter positions. Barbuda shook his head, and motioned for them to return to the car.

He looked around, above the crowd. He was in Habana Centro.

"Recognize this area?"

"Of course," he replied, looking up at the pinkish walls of the building in front of him, and the "Hotel Lincoln" blue lettering. "I remember this place, in fact. Used to be very popular, back when this was the popular part of the city."

"Shall we go in for a drink, and give them an honor to rejuvenate business?"

"I haven't had a drink in a long time."

He could already hear screeching tires and screaming engines, the security detail storming back, guns drawn and trigger fingers tense. They would probably grab hold of him, hurl him into a backseat, and speed off to safety without hesitation, just as they trained. He had a minute at most, to follow the spirit inside.

"I haven't had a drink in a long time."

* * * *

Sandra lay on her side, diagonally on the bed. She had untucked the towel when she returned to her room, letting it fall to the floor, and lay naked, with randomly placed rays of sunlight shooting through gaps in the window blinds, dotting and streaking her arms and thighs. Propping up on an elbow, she looked down at the medallion gift, moving it to catch and reflect the light, redirecting the illumination toward the ceiling.

She pushed herself into a sitting position, reaching around with both hands, loosening the slip knot on the chord until she could slide it back over her head and her hair. She stood, moved to the doll with the porcelain face, and readjusted the necklace to fit around it. Then Sandra picked up the towel from the floor, stepping quietly out and across to the bathroom. She wanted to take a long shower, and was hoping for some hot water.

The End

978-0-595-48618-2
0-595-48618-5